200

ghosts go *haunting*

books by
    sorche nic leodhas

ghosts go *haunting*

by sorche nic leodhas

illustrated by nonny hogrogian

holt, rinehart and winston

new york · chicago · san francisco

for richard keith digby

Library of Congress Catalog Card Number: 65-10349

96061-0915
Printed in the United States of America

Young America Book Club Edition

This edition is published by arrangement
with Holt, Rinehart and Winston, Inc.

contents

introduction

In my early days I was perplexed that while there were hundreds and hundreds of ghost stories, there were very few persons who would admit to a belief in ghosts. After giving much thought to the matter, I decided that the reason people thought they didn't believe in ghosts was because they had never happened to meet any. I am certain that every one of these doubters would have believed at once if he had met a ghost.

At about the same time I became convinced of something extraordinary. There are some people who seem to have invisible tentacles with which they reach out and draw to themselves others who have some knowledge of ghosts. Experience has proved to me that I am among the attracters of ghost-story tellers. It has been going on for so long that I cannot remember when people started to seek me out to tell me news of the supernatural world. I'd not be surprised at all if I were to learn that it began while I was still in my cradle. At any rate, it couldn't have been much later, for ghost stories are among my earliest memories. My conviction is strengthened by the fact that people still bring me news of ghosts. All these ghost-story tellers have one significant trait in common. They all believe what they are telling me is true, and they want me to believe it, too. Maybe the eerie experience was not their own, but they knew somebody who knew the man or woman it happened to, and they can bring up a battery of proof in the form of names and geographical locations. If you haven't met a ghost yourself, and if you are going to join the ranks of the believers, the next best thing is to meet one at second- or even third-hand.

Someone will come along and engage you in quite an ordinary conversation; right in the middle of it the ghost will pop in. The teller will probably say suddenly, "What you're saying calls to my mind old Ian Frazier. Him that was the cousin of the man that met the ghost at Doune." Then, in the most exasperating way, the teller will go off on another tack, so that you have to pursue the ghost through the conversation, bringing the teller back to the point whenever he wanders off. In the end, all you have are the bare bones of a ghost story. These you must clothe with the flesh of words, rounding, smoothing, and polishing. That is what makes a story. Quite often the persons who bring me ghost stories are strangers who tell their tales and go away and are never met again.

Take the way I happened to get the tale of "The Man Who Helped Carry the Coffin," for example. When I was living in New York the docks on the East River held a peculiar fascination for me. On my free days I used to go down to see if anything interesting was going on. Once in a while a ship that still sailed under canvas would be docked there. One lucky day I found a lumber schooner at one of the docks. Leaning against a rail above the water at the wharf-side, well out of the way of the men who were unloading her, I stood and watched the activity on her deck.

An old man appeared from somewhere and came to lean on the rail beside me. He bade me "Good day" politely, and we exchanged a few remarks about the ship. His voice had a good thick Scottish burr to it. It pleased my ears to hear it so I laid myself out to keep him talking. We talked of the sea, we talked of cargoes, and then I praised the day's weather, which was remarkably clear and bright. At that he shook his head doubtfully and said in the words Andrew MacQuarrie used in the story, "I dinna like the looks o't. The lift is is too blue and the breeze is too uncertain." Then he pointed out that all the birds were flying inland, away from the sea.

" 'Tis a sure sign of a storm on the way," he told me. "'Twas after sic a day the big storm came tae Dornock Bay. 'Twas that same nicht that Andrew MacQuarrie helpit tae carry the coffin." That was the way it began. I went after the story, and bit by bit, I got it. I never saw the old man again. But he was right about the weather. That night New York was struck by one of its most notable storms, for all the world like the one on Dornoch Bay.

A very good place to get news of ghosts is at the clan outings held annually in many of the large towns and cities in the United States. The clans take over a park or grove for the day, and gather together there. The atmosphere is so thickly Scottish you could cut it with a knife.

The sound and the color and the stir of a clan gathering is beyond believing. There is the brave show of the kilts of the men of the various clans. Kilts, of course, are purely men's attire. Scottish women never wear them. There is the sound of Scottish voices with the burr of the braid Scots, and now and then the soft singing cadence of the Gaelic. There is the wild music of the bagpipes, the roll and beat of the drums, and the rhythmic sound of the complicated footwork of the dancers treading out the reels, the strathspeys, the bobbs, and that ancient Scottish war-dance, more commonly known as the sword dance. And there will be the old songs and ballads, sorrowful or canty (merry), some of which have been handed down for hundreds of years.

Even the food at a clan outing is peculiarly Scottish, made from treasured recipes carried across the sea. There will be heaps and piles galore of mutton pasties, pork pies, Scotch eggs, sausage rolls, scones (with plenty of fresh butter and black currant jam to go with them), girdle bread, ginger cake, shortbread, Dundee rock, cold plum dumpling, Forfarshire tea cakes, fruit cake and the like, with lashings of good hot strong tea to wash it all down.

Where could a better place be found to get wind of a Scottish ghost?

All the stories in *Ghosts Go Haunting* came out of clan outings with the exception of two. One of these, of course, is "The Man Who Carried the Coffin," which I had from the old man I met by the East River dock. The other is "The Ghost That Didn't Want to Be a Ghost." That was one of my father's stories, but I can't tell you where he got it. He never said.

I didn't go to any trouble to get these stories. I just waited, knowing that sooner or later someone would come along and tell me about a ghost. Me being one of those attracters of ghost-tale tellers, why wouldn't they? And someone always does.

one

the wicked house of duncan macbain

After old Duncan MacBain was dead folks for miles around said that it was not a bad thing at all that he was gone. The world was well rid of him, they said. The fact that he died in a terrible fire that consumed him and his house and a dozen of his boon companions did not incline them to a kindlier opinion. Folks all agreed that his end was a judgment upon him because of his evil ways in this world, and a foretaste of what was coming to him in the next. The house was a wicked house, they said, and needed to be destroyed, and his friends who died with him were no better nor fitter for mercy than himself.

Evil reputations live on long after those who bore them have departed. Years after Duncan MacBain and his house and his friends had crumbled together into ashes, and the ruins were covered over by grass and brush and queer twisted dark trees, no one came near the place because its reputation for wickedness persisted. No sheep ever fed on the lush coarse grass nourished by the hidden ashes. No cattle ever watered at the spring by the tumble-down wall. No old body gathering fagots for a sheiling hearth ever ventured to add one branch from the stunted trees to her bundle. And folks making their way home after nightfall, rather than pass the place in the darkness, went a mile or two out of their way by another road.

Even by day the road which wandered away up the mountain at the right-hand side of the village, was seldom used, and then only by strangers who had never heard tell of Duncan MacBain. Of course, if a stranger had been foolhardy enough to want to go over old Duncan's road by night, the village folks would have done their best to hold him back. But by good fortune, strangers were few, and seemed contented enough to travel by day or, if benighted, they chose of their own accord to stay for the night in the village inn.

It was not to be expected that things would continue to go as smoothly as that. The trouble came when the government sent a young fellow up from London to make some sort of survey or other. He was a fine young laddie, and very full of himself. In no time at all he made himself felt in the place. At the inn, he told them he'd be needing the room no longer than a fortnight for it was not his habit to be wasting any of his time. He'd thank them to have his breakfast always ready for him at daybreak, and they could hold his dinner back until dark. He'd made it his practice to use all the hours of daylight, which was why he could get a job over and done with quicker than the next man. Or so he said.

The innkeeper and his wife were not unwilling, although it put them out a bit to keep his dinner over from noon till night and still have it fit to eat. But if he wanted it that way, he could have it. It did bother the innkeeper's wife to see him going off at the sgreuch o' dawn with naught but a bit of a cold piece for his midday dinner. The lad had need of a good hot meal at least once in the day, she said. So she did the best she could to see he got it.

Well, five or six days went by and he came in one night as cocky as ever. "Who lives in the big old house?" he asked. "The one two miles or so along the road up the mountain?"

The innkeeper looked puzzled. He shook his head. "I'd not be saying I know the house you're speiring about."

Some of the villagers who had dropped in for a friendly glass and a bit of news came in from the bar side of the room to join in the conversation. " 'Twould not be the crofter's bothan over by the crossroads?" one of them asked. "Only 'tis not two miles. A mile it would be—no more than that."

"There's the church with the manse by it," said another. "The manse is none so small. But it's not so far away as the crofter's bothan."

"I know the manse," said the young government man. "This house I'm talking about is not the manse. It's not the crofter's cottage, or bothan, or whatever you like to call it. I saw it as I came by tonight. Funny I never noticed it before. It wasn't dark yet, but the whole place was lit up from ground to roof as if they were having a ball. Besides, it isn't on the same road as the manse. It's on the other road. The one to the right up the mountain."

The village folks looked at one another uneasily, and then they looked away. Nobody said a word for several minutes. Then the innkeeper asked, "What road would you be meaning?"

"I just told you," the young man answered impatiently. "The road directly east from here. The one on the right-hand side of the village that goes straight up the mountain."

The innkeeper sighed heavily. "Och, aye," he said slowly. "Well, then. There is no house on that road. None at all!"

"None at all," agreed the rest of them. One man added hopefully. "Happen you're mixed a wee bit in your directions. There's Major MacNair's house stands two miles or more along, on the road to the north. It's not so easy to see from the road, for it's set back and there are some trees around it. But it's a fine big house."

The government man was beginning to lose his temper. "Do you think I don't know what I'm talking about?" he cried out angrily. "It's not the north road. The north road runs through the valley. It's the road that goes over the mountain on the right of the village. I ought to know. I just came down it. Do you think I don't know a house when I see it?"

Nobody said a word to that. To tell the truth, they had

no answer they wanted to give him, as they showed by slipping away into the bar again. The innkeeper followed them
shortly after, and left the young government man sitting
alone in the private bar and still very angry.

When they were sure he could not overhear them, the
men from the village got together in a corner by the door.
All of them whispered the same thing.

" 'Twas the wicked house o' auld Duncan MacBain,"
they all said, looking over their shoulders fearfully.

"Och, aye!"

"Och, aye. 'Twas that he was seeing!"

"What other house would it be?" asked the innkeeper.
"And it on a road that has no house from beginning to end?"

When the young fellow started out next morning, the
innkeeper blocked his way at the door.

"You'll not be going up the mountain, now?" asked
the innkeeper. "I'm thinking 'twould be well if you kept to
the valley this day."

The young man looked surprised. "It would not make
sense for me to do that. I can't quit a job in the middle of it."

"Well, then," the innkeeper said earnestly. "You'll do
well to take the road over that way," and he turned and
pointed to the left.

"Nonsense! It's much farther by that road. Why should
I go that way?" asked the young man.

"Och, no reason at all! No reason at all!" the innkeeper

answered hastily. "But the day has the look of a storm in it. The road to the right isn't one to travel over in bad weather. 'Tis not safe at all."

"I'll chance it," said the young fellow.

So the innkeeper gave up the argument and moved out of his way. The young government man went off in a huff, straight up the road to the right, determined to have his own way.

The innkeeper had been right about a storm brewing. It threatened all day, but it was not until late afternoon that it struck. The young man had never seen a Scottish storm before and its fury amazed him. For a minute he considered taking the innkeeper's advice and making his way across to the other road, but he was too stubborn to give in.

"Bosh!" he exclaimed. "How can one road be more dangerous than another?"

So he resigned himself to the long wet journey ahead of him. He pulled his coat collar up to his ears and his hat brim down over his eyes, and plodded along down the road through the storm. The rain poured down in cataracts and the thunder rolled across the sky, with a shaft of lightning now and then a bit too close for comfort. He was soon soaked to the skin and chilled to the bone. Before long he began to wish he'd taken the other road, after all. He hadn't seen so much as a shepherd's hut on this one, while along the other road he knew there were a number of places where people lived.

Someone would have let him take shelter from the storm there.

He was so wet and cold and so thoroughly miserable that the house was a great surprise to him when he saw it again. He stopped in the road and stared at it.

"No house indeed!" he exclaimed scornfully. "Then what would they call that?"

There it stood, just as he had seen it the night before, four full stories tall, and every window from ground to roof blazing with light. Just at that moment the front door was suddenly flung open and a man appeared at the head of the flight of steps that led up to the door. He held a glass in one hand and beckoned with the other.

"Come away in, lad!" he called in a loud jovial voice. "Come away in out of the cold and the rain. You'll be finding it warm and dry enough inside!"

The young man needed no second invitation. He turned away from the road and hurried across the grass toward the house where warmth and good cheer waited for him. He never knew what it was that made him stop just before he reached the steps and look up to the man at the top, and through the open door behind him. Whatever it was, the sight he saw gave him the shock of his life.

To his horror he saw that what he had taken for lights was blazing fire! *The house was full of it!*

As he stood there, terror-stricken, a great burst of flame

came rolling down the steps straight at him. He covered his eyes with his arms and flung himself face down upon the ground. He could feel the heat of it coming closer. He heard the great, shattering, hollow sound of a terrible explosion—and then he heard and felt nothing more.

When the storm had passed over and the young government man did not come back for his supper, the innkeeper and his wife began to grow uneasy. As hour after hour went by and he did not return, they became more and more anxious about him, and by midnight the innkeeper had fretted himself into a terrible state. So around the village he went, calling all the men out of their beds to come with him to hunt the missing man.

There was a lot of headshaking and grumbling when they found out that they were expected to go up old Duncan MacBain's road to search for the young surveyor, but finally the innkeeper persuaded them that they would come to no harm as long as they kept close together. It helped a bit that the village doctor led the way with his old horse and carriage. The doctor put no stock in ghosts and said so bluntly. But he thought maybe the poor lad would have need of his services, which was why he came along.

They found him easily enough, and how could they miss him, with every man of them carrying a lantern, and with the moon after the storm riding the sky and flooding the land with light? He lay at the foot of the grassy mound

where the house of old Duncan MacBain once stood. At first they thought he was dead but the doctor looked him over and said there was still life in him.

When after some time and trouble the doctor brought him to his senses again, he sat up and called out wildly, "Fire! Fire! The house is on fire!"

"What house?" asked the doctor calmly as he packed up his bag. "De'il a house is here, my lad."

The young man looked about him. There was no house there, to be sure. All that he saw by the lantern light and the moonlight was the grassy mound and the stunted dark trees and the tumble-down wall.

"Och, 'twas the ghost of a house you saw," said one of the searchers who were all huddled close together by the place where once the gate had been.

"Och, aye!" the others agreed. "The ghost of the house of old Duncan MacBain."

"Havers!" the doctor said gruffly. " 'Twas naught but a shock from lightning striking near him. But you'll have this lad's own ghost on your hands if you leave him to lie out here much longer."

None of them wanted any more ghosts about the neighborhood, so they hurried him into the doctor's carriage and back to his bed at the inn. But they paid no heed to what the doctor said about lightning and shocks. They all knew better.

The young government man's work wasn't done in a fortnight after all. By the time he was able to be up and around again he'd lost his taste for getting out at daybreak, and he'd become used to having a good hot midday dinner. It suited him fine to work on some of his reports in the morning and go out to work after he'd eaten his meal at noon. He began to come back earlier, too, well before dusk set in.

It slowed him up a bit, but that didn't seem to bother him. So he was around the village for quite a long time. Folks got to know him and began to like him, for all that he was a Sassenach born and bred. Everybody noticed that he was never so cocksure or so full of himself as he had been when he came. Another thing they noticed was that whether he had finished his job there that last day or not, he never again went up the mountain, by any road at all. He'd seen all he wanted to see of the wicked house of old Duncan MacBain.

two

the man who didn't believe in ghosts

In a town not far from Edinburgh there was a house that was said to be haunted. It wasn't the sort of house you'd think would attract a ghost at all. It was only a two-story cottage with a garret, and it was far too neat and pretty for ghosts to care much about. The outside walls of it were painted white and its casement windows had diamond-shaped panes to them. There was a climbing rose trained over the front door, and there was a flower garden before the house and a kitchen garden behind it, with a pear tree and an apple tree and a small green lawn. Who'd ever think that a ghost would choose to bide in a place like that? But folks did say it was haunted, all the same.

The house had belonged to an old attorney with only one child, a daughter. Folks old enough to remember her still say that there never was another lass as bonny as her in the town. The old man loved her dearly but she died early. There was an old sad story told about her being in love with the son of an old laird who did not favor the match. The poor lad died of a fever while they were still courting, and not long after she died too—folks said of a broken heart.

After that the old man lived alone in the house, with a

woman coming in each day to take care of it. There wasn't a word said about ghosts in the old man's time. He'd not have put up with it for a minute.

When the old attorney died, there was nobody left that was kin to him but a second cousin several times removed. So to keep the property in the family, the old man left all he had to the cousin, including the house, of course.

The young man was grateful, but as he was not married, he had little use for a house. The lodgings he was living in suited him fine. So he put the renting of the house into an agent's hands. The rent money would make a nice little nest egg against the time when he decided he would like to get married. When that time came he'd want the house for himself.

It was the folks the agent found to live in the house that started all the talk about ghosts. At first they were very well pleased with the house, but as time passed they began to notice queer things were happening in it. Doors would open and close again, with nobody at all near them. When the young wife was dusting the spare bedroom, she heard drawers being pulled open and shut again behind her, but when she turned about to look, no one at all was there.

Things were lifted and put down again before the tenants' very eyes, but they couldn't see who was lifting them or putting them down. They came to have the feeling that there was somebody always in the house with them. Of course, they tried to be sensible about it, but it gave them a terribly eerie feeling. As for getting a maid to stay, it couldn't be done! The maids all said that they felt that someone was always looking over their shoulders while they worked, and every time they set something down, it got itself moved to another place. They wouldn't take it upon themselves to say why, but they'd take whatever pay was coming to them, and go. And they did.

The end of the tenants' stay in the house came upon the day when the young wife came into the sitting room to find her wee lad rolling his ball across the floor. Every time the ball reached the middle of the room it seemed to turn and roll itself back to him, as if someone who couldn't be seen were playing with him. But when he looked up at his mother and laughed and said "Bonny lady!" 'twas more than she could bear. She caught him up in her arms and ran out of the door to one of the neighbors, and no one could persuade her to set foot in the house again. So her husband went to the agent and told him they were sorry, but the way things were, they'd have to give up the house.

The young man to whom the house had been left was a very matter-of-fact young fellow. He didn't believe in ghosts. He was quite put out because the story had got around that there were ghosts in the house. Of course, the young couple who had lived there couldn't be depended on not to talk about what had happened. It wouldn't have been according to

human nature for them to keep quiet about it. What made it awkward was that by this time the young man had found a lass he wanted to marry, but unfortunately she had heard the story. And she did believe in ghosts.

She said that she loved him dearly and would like very much to marry him. But she told him flatly that she could never, *never* bring herself to live in a haunted house.

Then the young man told her that he would go and live in the house himself, just to prove that there were no ghosts in it. Anyway, he didn't believe in ghosts. So he left his lodgings and moved in and got himself settled comfortably in his house.

Well, the doors did open and close of themselves, but that didn't daunt him. He just took them off their hinges and rehung them. They went on opening and closing just the same, but he said that was only because of a flaw in the walls.

He had to admit to himself that he heard drawers opening and closing, and latches of cupboards clicking shut. There was a tinkling in the china closet, too, as if someone were moving the cups and plates about. And once or twice he thought he heard water running in the scullery. But when he looked, every tap was shut off tight. Besides, he knew there was no one but himself in the house. So he said that old houses were always full of queer noises because of the foundations settling, and paid them no more heed.

Even when a book he had just closed and laid on the table opened itself again, and the leaves turned over slowly as if someone were looking at them, he told himself that it was just a puff of wind from the window did it, although afterward he remembered that the windows were closed at the time.

But still he didn't believe in ghosts.

So he went on living in the house and trying to persuade his sweetheart to marry him and come and live there with him. And, of course, to convince her that the house wasn't haunted at all. But he had no luck, for she wouldn't be persuaded.

Well, things went on in this unsatisfactory way until his summer holidays came around. He decided, now that he had the time for it, to do something he'd been meaning to do and never got around to. There were a lot of clothes in the attic that had belonged to the old lawyer and his daughter. It seemed sinful to leave them there to moulder away when some poor body'd be glad to have them. So what he was going to do was to pack them all up and send them to the Missionary Society where a good use would be found for them.

He went up to the garret and found some empty boxes, and began to pack the clothes. They were all hanging in tall presses, ranged around the room. He packed the old lawyer's clothes first. There were a good many of them, suits and coats and boots and shoes, all of the best quality, to say nothing of a quantity of warm underclothing in boxes neatly stacked on the floors of the presses. When he had taken everything out and folded it neatly, he packed the boxes and set them out of his way, and turned to the press that held the dead lass's clothes. When he opened the first press there was a sound uncommonly like a sigh. It gave him a start for a moment, but then he laughed and told himself that it was only the silk of garments brushing against each other in the breeze made by the opening door. He began to take them out, one by one, and to fold them and gently lay them in the box he'd set ready for them. It made him feel a little bit sad and sentimental to be handling the dresses that had been worn by the pretty young thing who had died so young and so long ago.

He'd laid away five or six of them when he came to one frock that seemed strangely heavy for the material of which it was made. It was a light, crisp cotton sprigged with flowers still bright in spite of the years it had hung in the press. He thought that a dress like that should have had almost no weight at all, so he looked it over curiously. Perhaps a brooch or a buckle was the answer? Then he found a pocket set in the seam of the skirt, and in the pocket a small red book and a letter. It was a letter of the old style, with no envelope, and the dead girl's name and address on the outer folded sheet. He laid the dress aside and, taking his find to the low-set window, he sat down on the floor to read what he had found. He was not a man to read other people's letters and secrets, but something made him feel that it was right to do so now.

He read the letter first. It said:

My dear love:

Although they have not told me I know that I am very ill. It may be that we shall not meet again in this world. If I should die I beg of you to make them promise that when you, too, are dead we shall lie together side by side.

Your true love.

The young man sat for a while, thinking of the letter, wondering how it had come to the lass, remembering that he had heard that the old laird was dead set against the match. Then he took up the little red book and opened it. The little book was a sort of day-by-day diary with the date printed at the top of each page. It had begun as a sort of housekeeping journal. There was a lot in it about household affairs. There were records of sewing done, of jars of pickles and jams laid by, and about the house being turned out and cleaned from end to end, and such things. But through it all was the story of a young girl's heart. She told about meeting the laird's son, where they first met and when he first spoke to her of love and what they said and how they planned to marry as soon as the old laird could be persuaded to give his consent to the match. Although he was against it, they thought he might be brought over in time.

But they had no time, poor young things! Soon after, the diary told of the letter that John the Carrier had brought her, that had frightened her terribly. And the next page said only, "My love is dead." Page after page was empty after that. Then toward the end of the little book she had written: "I know that I am going to die. I asked my father today to promise to beg the laird to let me lie beside my love when I am dead, but he only turned away and would not answer. I am afraid his pride will not let him ask a favor of one who would not accept me into his family. But, oh my love, if he does not, I'll find a way to bring things right. I'll never rest until I do."

And that was all.

The young man raised his eyes from the page and repeated thoughtfully, "I'll never rest until I do."

It was right then and there that he began to believe in ghosts!

He put the diary and the letter into his pocket, and leaving everything just as it was in the garret, he went downstairs. The packing could wait for another day. He had something better to do. As he went he thought of the old attorney living there day after day with the ghost of his dead daughter mutely beseeching him to do what his pride would never let him do.

"Well, I have no pride at all," the young man said.

He packed a bag and put on his hat and coat, and started

for the station. But as he went out the door, he turned and put his head back in and called out, "Do not fret yourself any longer, lass! You can rest now. I'll find the way to bring things right."

At the station he was fortunate enough to find a train that would take him where he wanted to go. When he got off the train he asked about the village for news of the laird. Och, the old laird was long dead, folks told him, and a rare old amadan that one was, though they shouldn't be saying it of the dead. But the new laird, him that was the old laird's nephew, had the estate now, and a finer man you'd not be finding should you search for a year and a day.

So up to the castle the young man went. When he got there he found the new laird as reasonable a man as he could hope to find. So he gave him the letter and the diary and let him read the story for himself. Then he told him about his house and the ghost in it that would not rest until she had her way.

The old laird's nephew listened gravely, and at the end of the young man's story he sighed and said, "Fifty years! Fifty long years! What a weary time to wait. Poor lass."

The old laird's nephew believed in ghosts himself.

He called his solicitors at once and got them to work. They were so quick about it that by the time the young man got back home after paying a visit to the old laird's nephew who asked him to stay till all was settled, the two lovers were reunited at last and lay together side by side in the old laird's family tomb.

When he got home he could tell the minute he stepped through the door that there was no one there but himself. There was no more trouble with the doors, and the only sounds were the ordinary sounds that he made himself.

He finally persuaded the lass he wanted to marry to come for supper one night and bring along the old aunt she lived with. The aunt prided herself on having such a keen scent for ghosts that she could actually smell one if it was in a house. So they came, and as soon as they were all settled at the supper table the aunt looked all around the room and sniffed two or three times.

"Ghosts! Nonsense, my dear!" she said to the young man's lass firmly. "There isn't a single ghost in this house. You may be sure I'd know at once, if there were!"

That satisfied the young lady. So, soon she and the young man were married. They lived together so happily in the house that folks completely forgot that it had ever been said that it was haunted. It didn't look at all like the kind of a house that would ever have a ghost. Only the young man remembered.

He really did believe in ghosts, after all.

three

the man who walked widdershins
round the kirk

When you go around anything you want to be sure to go clockwise—that is, the way the hands of a clock travel, from right to left. That's what the Scots call "going deasil." If you go the other way, you're going backward, from left to right, and that is called "going widdershins," and it's a dangerous thing to do for it's bound to bring you bad luck.

There was once a young man who lived in a village t'other side of Galashiels who walked widdershins round a kirk, and a terrible experience he got from it. It wasn't because he didn't know any better. He'd heard his mother and his grandmother and other old folks talk about it many a time. The trouble with him was that he was one of the sort that is so stubborn and so set upon going their own gait that the only way to steer them is to tell them to go the other way. Then you can be sure they'll go the way you want them to go.

The name of this lad was Alistair MacGillivray, but everybody called him Sandy. One day Sandy and a friend of his were taking a shortcut through the kirkyard. They had to go around the kirk to reach the path they were going to take beyond it. When they got to the corner of the kirkyard near the building, Sandy turned to the right to go around it.

"Och, nay, Sandy!" his friend exclaimed, forgetting for a minute that Sandy wouldn't take a telling. "You cannot go round the kirk that direction."

"Why not, then?" asked Sandy.

"It's widdershins that way," his friend protested.

"What of it?" Sandy said. "It's shorter than going round the other way. Come along, lad!"

But his friend held back. "I'd not have the dare, Sandy. It would just be asking for trouble, to walk widdershins. Especially round the kirk. You can't do it."

"I can, indeed," said Sandy, growing more stubborn every minute. "And what's more, I will. I'll walk widdershins the whole way round just to show you. You watch me!"

So Sandy went off to the front of the church and made a sharp turn to the right side of it, whistling a tune like a lark to show he didn't care at all. He turned at the corner and went along the right side of the kirk. Then across the back he went and down the other side, going widdershins all the way.

When he turned the last corner and came back to the front of it, he found his friend standing there in the kirkyard waiting for him and looking awful scared.

"Well, then, I did it," Sandy said triumphantly, starting to walk over to his friend. But just then he set his foot down right on the place he started out from and poof! He disappeared!

He was there one minute and the next minute he wasn't, just like a candle flame blown out by the wind.

His friend blinked and his jaw dropped and he stared at the empty space where Sandy had just been standing. Then he gave a great screech and turned about and raced off to the village to spread the news that something awful had happened to Sandy MacGillivray.

Sandy did not realize at all that anything strange had happened to him, though he did have a queer sort of feeling that he couldn't quite explain. His friend had behaved as if he had suddenly gone daft, and Sandy was terribly puzzled about it. He went over to the low wall that ran around the kirkyard and sat down on top of it to think things over and try to figure out what had made his friend go off shrieking in such a daft way.

While he was sitting there and thinking, with his hands lying loose-like on his knees, Sandy happened to let his eyes fall upon them. He got a horrible fright. Losh! He had no hands! Nor any knees, nor any legs or feet! In fact, he had no body at all, as far as he could see. Then Sandy understood what had happened to him. *He'd turned into a ghost!* It all came from walking widdershins round the kirk.

The worst of it was that he wasn't even a proper ghost, with a corpse that had been waked by his friends and buried. He was a ghost without even a grave that he could call his own. Och, poor Sandy MacGillivray was in a sad, sad state.

Well, he was sitting there feeling sorry for himself and wondering what he was to do about it, when he heard a lot of clamor from the road. A crowd of folks from the village came tearing up to the kirkyard with his friend at the head of them leading the way.

They all poured into the kirkyard and began looking about among the gravestones for Sandy, calling him by name. They didn't believe what Sandy's friend had told them about the way Sandy had vanished. All of them were sure that they'd be finding him hiding somewhere. 'Twas just the sort of fala-dha Sandy'd like to play on them, and him being always ready for a joke.

They paid no heed to Sandy, sitting on the kirkyard wall, which was not surprising, since they couldn't see him. After he'd called out to them a couple of times to tell them where to find him, he discovered that they couldn't hear him either. So he gave up trying and just sat there on the wall watching them hunting for him and feeling very low in his spirits.

When they had called and hunted for a long while without finding hide or hair of Sandy, they began to tell one another that maybe Sandy's friend was right, and Sandy had vanished after all. At any rate they were tired of hunting for him and they might as well go back to the village. For some reason or other they didn't feel comfortable in the kirkyard after what had happened to Sandy MacGillivray there.

They stood for a while talking about Sandy just outside the kirkyard. Sandy was so near to them he could have leaned out and touched them if he wanted. He didn't bother because he thought they wouldn't feel his touch. He had to grin to think of the fright he could give them if they could. But then he heard his name spoken and began to listen to what was being said.

"I told him not to walk widdershins," Sandy's friend lamented. "I told him, but he wouldn't heed me."

"And you the fool of the world to tell him that!" said one of the searchers. "And you knowing Sandy the way you do."

" 'Twas the worst thing you could do," said another. "Tell Sandy to do one thing and you might be sure he'd do the very opposite. Where were your wits, lad?"

"I wouldn't want to be saying a word against Sandy now that he's no longer with us—in a manner of speaking," said another in a pious tone. But he spoiled it by adding, "But I'll tell you this. I never saw a stubborner lad or one that was more contrary!"

It shocked Sandy quite a bit to hear how quick the others were to agree with the speaker. "Och, aye!" "Och, aye!" they said as they went down the road.

So there was poor Sandy MacGillivray, a ghost but not a proper ghost, left sitting all alone on the kirkyard wall.

He'd never thought about himself before, or about what folks might think of him, but now he spent a long time turning what he'd heard about himself over in his mind. He had to admit that there was naught but truth in it. Stubborn he'd been and contrary he'd been, and he was in a terrible fix because of it.

What was he going to do now? He didn't like to go home because, ghost or not, he was sure his mother would know him, and it would give her a terrible fright. He wouldn't go to the village because folks would be gathered around talking about him, and like as not he wouldn't care at all for what they'd say. But he couldn't go on sitting here on the churchyard wall, because after dark there might be other ghosts in the place, and Sandy was afraid of ghosts—proper ghosts, that is. What in the world was he going to do?

Then it came into his mind that since he'd got into trouble going around the kirk the wrong way, maybe going around it the right way would do him some good. Anyway, it was worth trying.

So he got down off the wall and went up to the front of the kirk and started off again. But this time he went the right way, from right to left, clockwise, going deasil all the way. He came slowly around the last corner and up to the front of the kirk so scared that it wouldn't work that he could scarcely breathe. But the minute he set his foot on the place he'd started out from he felt a great shock that shook him from head to foot. He looked down at himself, and there he was again! Sandy MacGillivray, all his own self, flesh and blood and bones again.

Sandy patted his shoulders and his arms and his legs, and clapped his hands for joy. Och, 'twas a rare grand thing, so it was, to have a body back again.

When he got home his mother was setting food upon the table. She said to Sandy, "The supper's ready. Will you have it, Sandy?" She was expecting Sandy to say, "Och, I'm not wanting it now." Or else, "Nay, I'll take my supper later," Sandy always being so contrary.

But Sandy gave her the surprise of the world. He slipped into his own place across from his father. "Aye," said Sandy meekly, "I'll have my supper now."

While he was eating his supper up came his friend with a deputation of lads from the village. They all looked solemn and mournful for they'd come to tell Sandy's family that Sandy had disappeared. When they saw him sitting there they couldn't believe their eyes.

"Is it yourself, Sandy?" they all cried as they gathered around him.

"Aye," said Sandy calmly. "Who else would it be?"

Sandy's friend could never explain it. Sandy never said a word. Folks began to say that Sandy's friend had dreamed it all. He had to take so much of their joking about it that sometimes he wished that he had disappeared himself.

One good thing came of it. It cured Sandy MacGillivray of being stubborn and contrary. Sandy was a changed man. And never, never, never again in all his days did Sandy MacGillivray walk widdershins around a kirk.

four

the tale the crofter told

One of the strangest tales that ever came out of the Highlands was told by a crofter who lived beyond Invercannich. He and his wife were young folks when it happened, and they were the ones it happened to.

It's lonely country there and always has been. There's no town nearby and only the shepherds' bothans along the way, while the crofts are few and far between.

The crofter and his wife didn't mind the loneliness. They had each other, and three bairns all as hearty and happy as ever you'd hope to see. Besides, the young couple were getting a good start in life. They had their own place and a fair-sized flock of sheep, to say nothing of a cow and a good small horse. Their three laddies had no need to feel lonely because they had each other for company. The wife's young brother was with them, too. He had come from Invercannich to bide at the croft and give them a hand with the sheep. There was plenty of work about the place to keep them all occupied so they were too busy to think about being lonely.

Well, days came and days went by, all very much the same. Then one night the wife woke the crofter. She said to him, "Whisht! I hear a babe greeting!"

The crofter was tired and wanted his sleep, so he answered, "Leave be, lass! 'Tis one of the bairns greeting in his sleep."

"Nay," said she, " 'tis no bairn of our own. 'Tis not in the house at all."

By this time the crofter was wide awake and none too pleased about it. "A night bird, then," he said crossly. "Will ye not hold your whisht and go back to sleep?"

Then he heard it himself. It did sound like a bairn crying somewhere outside. But it stopped all of a sudden and then they heard a voice, very soft and low, singing a lullaby.

"Och, 'tis only Wully amusing himself up on the mountainside," the crofter said. His wife's brother, Wully, was taking his turn by night with the sheep.

"That hasn't the sound o' Wully's voice. 'Tis more like a woman's," the crofter's wife insisted.

"Och, what woman would be going along, and her with a bairn, at this hour of the night?" the crofter demanded. " 'Tis only Wullie up to some trick or other, you may be sure."

She said no more, although he could tell well that she was not satisfied. But after a while they got back to sleep again.

When Wully came in with the pail of milk in the morn he said, "Happen the cow is going dry."

"She couldn't be!" the crofter's wife protested.

"Someone's been milking her then," Wully said. "There's not so much milk as yestermorn, by far." And he held the pail down for her to see.

"Och, Wully, you're teasing," the wife said. "You'll have been drinking it your own self."

"That I did not!" Wully told her. "You know well that I do not like cow's milk."

And so she did. Wully could never bear cow's milk, even as a child. Now if it were ewe's milk—or even goat's milk—he'd drink it gladly and like it fine. But never cow's milk. But what could be wrong that the cow did not give a full pail?

Then the crofter asked, "What way were you singing in the night, Wully?"

Wully turned surprised eyes upon him. "Singing?" he said. "Me? Och, I was not singing at all."

The crofter looked at the lad closely, but Wully's face was solemn and had the look of one telling the truth.

"I was whistling, though," Wully admitted. "It was when I was practicing my reel up on the flat stone." Shepherds often practiced their reels on the big stones that cropped out on the hillsides, getting ready for the contests at the fairs, while the sheep were at rest. "Och!" cried Wully. "I fear I was waking you. I did not mean to do so."

"Nay, nay, laddie," the shepherd said kindly. "We did not hear you at all."

"Did you hear naught in the night, Wully?" his sister asked.

"I thought I heard one of the bairns weeping," Wully said. "I could not tell for sure. The wind was blowing away from me."

"Our bairns slept the whole night through," said the crofter's wife. "They did not wake at all."

"Let's have no more havering about it," the crofter told them. "Whatever it was, 'tis no affair of ours. There's work to be done."

So they said no more about it.

But that night it happened again. The crofter's wife woke him and said, "Hear now? The bairn is greeting again." And all was the same. First the sound of the child crying, and then the voice singing soft and low. "Whoever can it be out there in the dark and all?"

"How would I be knowing?" the crofter answered impatiently. "Unless your brother Wully would be having his bit of fun with us."

"My brother Wully is not given to lying," the crofter's wife said reproachfully.

"Och, lass, I did not mean it. The lad's fine. But it is a queer old thing to be happening. I cannot explain it at all."

But by that time the voice had stopped singing. The only sound they heard was the night wind blowing across the thatch.

When Wully came in from milking the cow in the morn he said naught, but he held the pail for his sister to see. The milk was low in the pail again.

"I did not whistle last night," Wully told them.

"You could have done," said the crofter. " 'Twould not have waked us. We never heard you before."

"Och, aye," said Wully. "Maybe so." But he seemed to have something on his mind. After a while he said, "But I heard something in the night."

"What was it you heard?" the crofter's wife asked eagerly.

"I heard a bairn greeting," said Wully.

" 'Twas none of ours," said his sister. "Our bairns did not wake."

"Och, well and then I heard a woman singing bye-low to the bairn, and it stopped its greeting. And that was all."

"We heard the same," the crofter said.

"For two nights now we've heard it," said the crofter's wife.

"A woman with a bairn out there alone in the night!" cried Wully. "I watched and watched. It was bright moonlight and I saw nobody at all. *Where can they be?*"

Wully had asked the question for all of them; himself, the crofter, and his wife.

With no discussion at all, as if they shared each other's thoughts, the crofter and Wully rose from the table when the morning's meal was over and went out together to seek the woman and the bairn.

They did not come back until long after midday. Wully, worn out by his long night with the sheep and the morning's search, plodded silently off to his bed.

The crofter shook his head at the question in his wife's eyes. "There's nowhere we haven't looked," he told her wearily. "We went up the road and down the road for miles. We searched every bothan that was empty, and we asked every shepherd we met. Not a soul had seen them, nor heard them. There's not enough cover on the hill to hide anything bigger than a fox or a hare. I thought they might have taken shelter in one of our sheds, but they were not there. It's not canny!"

"Is it a spell laid on us?" whispered his wife, turning pale.

"I'd have thought the same," said the crofter. "Had Wully not found this." He held his hand out, open. His wife took what lay on his outstretched palm and looked at it.

" 'Tis a bairn's boot," she said. It was a small knitted boot of the sort mothers fashion for their bairns before they have reached the age to run about on their own two feet.

" 'Tis no witch-spell, then," she said slowly, turning it over in her hands and examining it closely. " 'Tis no witch-spell! Och, that is what I was fearing it would be!"

It was what the crofter had feared, too. But what bairn made up of a witch's moonshine spells would need a wee knitted boot to warm its feet?

"Where did Wully find it?" asked the crofter's wife.

"It was lying by the side of the road close by the path where the cow comes up to be milked," the crofter told her.

She stood for a minute thinking, then she laid the wee boot upon the shelf and turned to face her husband.

"If the bairn cries again in the night, I'll rise from my bed and go to him," she told him, "and neither you nor Wully nor Heaven itself will stop me."

The crofter had no wish to gainsay her. He only nodded and went about his work.

Neither the crofter nor his wife could sleep that night for listening. When the cry of the child came again in the night, the crofter's wife rose from her bed. She took her shawl and wrapped it about her and out of the door she went. Her husband hurried into his clothes and followed after her.

The moon was full and bright, and the night was clear and cloudless. The wife went up the road before him toward the field where they kept the cow. She stopped of a sudden, and stood looking intently through a gap in the hedge at something in the field. The crofter moved up beside her and looked over her shoulder to see what she was peering at.

There was a woman in the middle of the field kneeling beside the cow and milking it.

"Och!" the crofter muttered impatiently. "So that's who's been taking the milk!" And he made as if to go through the break in the hedge. But his wife caught his arm and held him back.

"Nay!" she whispered. "Bide a bit. She'll be carrying the milk to the bairn."

The woman stood up at the moment and started across the field away from them toward a tree that grew alone at the other side. 'Twas a big old tree, very old, and beginning to die of its age. In its trunk somewhat above the ground was a great hollow place. The woman walked steadily, but slowly and carefully, for in her hands she carried a bowl. When she got to the tree she took the bowl in one hand and reaching into the tree with the other she took a bairn out upon her arm. She held the cup to its lips to let it drink. The babe stopped crying and drank, and when it had finished the woman laid the bowl aside in the hollow of the tree. Then she

cradled the bairn in her arms and bent her head above it. Rocking it gently to and fro, she began to sing her lullaby.

"Och!" said the crofter. "What a great pair of ganders were Wully and me not to think of looking in the tree!"

But his wife was no longer beside him. She was running across the field so fast you'd have thought her feet had wings. And as she ran, she cried out, "Come, lass! Come into the house with your bairn!"

The woman stopped short in the middle of her song.

She made no move to run away, but stood still in the shadows under the tree, watching and waiting. She smiled when the crofter's wife came up to her, and held out the bairn. The crofter's wife took the child in her arms. In that same moment the woman was gone! It was not so much that she disappeared as that she seemed to dissolve before their eyes in cloudy wisps like the morning mist with the sun shining through it. But the bairn remained, nestling against the shoulder of the wife. It was warm and alive enough. There was no mistake about that.

Wully had seen his sister and her husband come out of the house and wondered what was amiss. He came pounding down the hill to join them. All they could do was show him the bairn. They were too badly shaken to put into words all that had happened. So they took the child back to the house with them and made a place for it there with their own weans.

Two or three days later a man came by seeking among the crofts for news of his sister. He said her husband had died some weeks before, and she had gone mad for grief, poor lass. He and his wife had tried to keep an eye on her, but the week before she had taken her babe and slipped away while they were asleep. When they showed him the bairn he knew it at once for his sister's child, and he said the bowl they had taken from the hollow tree was one from his own house.

They searched for the woman for days, but never found a

trace of her. There was a bad bit of bog beyond the tree where she gave them the bairn. She must have laid her bairn in the hollow of the tree and wandered into the bog searching for her husband and been swallowed up in the mire. But one thing they knew full well. 'Twas no living woman who put the babe in the arms of the crofter's wife. She had come back from the dead to tend to her child.

They wouldn't give up the bairn, for the crofter's wife said it was a trust given to her by its dead mother, and when she took it from her she had taken it into her heart. The man had a houseful of bairns of his own and not much to feed them and clothe them with, so he was willing for them to have it. So the crofter and his wife kept it and brought it up and loved it as well as if it were their own.

That's the tale the crofter told, and if you want proof of its truth you may stop at the croft beyond Invercannich and they'll show you the bowl they took from the hollow tree.

five

the wild ride in the tilt cart

There was a lad named Tommy Hayes and a more likable lad you'd never hope to see, for all that he was a Sassenach born and bred. Tommy was the sort to take his fishing very seriously, so when a Scottish friend wrote him and invited him to come up to his place in the Highlands for a visit and be sure to bring his fishing gear, Tommy was delighted. He'd always heard the fishing up where his friend lived was extra fine but he'd never had a chance to try it before. So right away he sent a telegram to his friend to say he was coming and what time they could expect him to get there. Then he packed up his fishing gear and a few clothes in his bag, and off he went.

He stepped off the train just about nightfall into the midst of a teeming rain with the water coming down in bucketsful and sloshing all over the place. The very first thing he discovered was that nobody had come to meet him. The station was on the edge of a small village, and there wasn't a soul in sight except for the stationmaster, and he was inside the station keeping out of the rain.

Tommy couldn't understand it for he'd sent the telegram in plenty of time. He went in and asked the stationmaster if he had seen anyone in the village from his friend's place, thinking maybe they'd had an errand to do and would be coming along for him later. But the stationmaster said that nobody at all had come over from that way for as good as a week. Tommy was surprised and maybe a little bit annoyed but he settled down in a corner of the station to wait for somebody to come and fetch him. He waited and waited and waited but nobody came at all, and after a while he found out why. The stationmaster came out of his bit of an office with a telegram in his hand. "This is for the folks up where you're going," he told Tommy. "Maybe you'd not mind taking it along, since you're going there yourself."

Tommy didn't have to read the telegram to know that it was the one he had sent to his friend. Well, that explained why nobody had come to meet his train. And what was more, nobody was going to come. Since the telegram hadn't been delivered, they wouldn't know at all that he was there.

"Och, well, 'tis a pity," said the stationmaster. " 'Twas early this morn I got it, and I'd have sent it along had anyone been passing by that was going in that direction. But what with the weather and all, there's few been out this day, and what there was, was bound the other way."

Well, being a good-natured lad, Tommy couldn't see any sense in making a fuss about it. He'd just have to find a way for himself to get where he wanted to go.

The stationmaster was sorry for Tommy, but he could

give him no help. There was nobody in the village who'd be able to take Tommy to his friend's house that night. Two or three of the folks had farm carts, but the beasts were all put up for the night and folks were all in their beds. They wouldn't be likely to take it kindly if Tommy woke them out of their sleep.

"You could stay in the station o'ernight," the man said. "You'd be welcome to do so, if you liked to. Happen there'll be someone along on the morrow going the way you want to go."

"And maybe not," said Tommy, not feeling very hopeful. "No, if I'm going to get there at all, I can see I'll have to walk."

"Aye," the stationmaster agreed. " 'Tis a matter of five miles."

"That's not too bad," said Tommy, determined to be cheerful.

"Mostly up and down hill," said the stationmaster glumly. "The road is rough, forbye. And 'tis raining."

"It can't be helped," said Tommy. "I'll just have to make the best of it." He picked up his bag and started out into the rain. The stationmaster came to the door and pointed out the road Tommy was to take. Tommy had gone a little way when the man called out after him. "Have a care for auld Rabbie MacLaren! I doubt he'll be out on the road the night."

That didn't mean a thing to Tommy, so he just plodded along through the rain.

The stationmaster had told him no lies about the road. Tommy couldn't remember having trod a worse one. It was up and down hill all right. Tommy toiled along, splashing through the puddles and slipping on loose pebbles with the rain pouring from the back of his hat brim down inside the collar of his coat. He was beginning to wonder if the fishing was going to be fine enough to pay for all the trouble he was going through to get it when he heard the sound of cart wheels rolling up the hill behind him.

He stopped and turned to look, and although it was growing dark he could make out the vague shape of a tilt cart coming toward him. It had a canvas top stretched over some sort of a framework, and Tommy thought to himself that if he could get a lift he'd be out of the rain at any rate. He set his bag down and stood in the middle of the road, waving his arms and shouting.

"Will you give me a lift up the road?" called Tommy.

The driver did not answer but the cart came on swiftly, bumping along over the ruts in a heedless way. As it came up to him, Tommy called out again. "Will you give me a lift?"

The man in the cart didn't say "Aye," but he didn't say "Nay." The cart kept on rolling along and Tommy had to pick up his bag and jump to the side of the road to keep from being run down.

"I'll pay you well," cried Tommy as he jumped. He felt rather desperate. The tilt cart was his only hope, for he doubted if he'd have another chance to get a lift that night. "I'll pay you well!" said Tommy again.

The driver did not answer, but it seemed to Tommy that the horse that was drawing the cart slowed down a little. Tommy took that as a sign that his offer had been accepted. He picked up his bag and ran after the cart and hopped in beside the driver without waiting for the cart to come to a full stop.

As soon as Tommy was in the cart the horse picked up speed again. The creature didn't seem to be minding the roughness of the road in the least. It brought the cart up to the crest of the hill at a good round pace and, when they started down the other side, the horse stretched its legs and fairly flew. The cart bounced and bumped and jolted over the ruts and Tommy's teeth chattered with the shaking he was getting. All he could do was hold fast to the side of the cart and hope for the best. The cart wheels threw out sparks as they hit the stones that strewed the road, and every now and then a big one sent the cart a foot or more in the air. Uphill and downhill went Tommy with the cart, hanging on for dear life and expecting to land any minute in a heap in the ditch with horse, cart, and driver piled on top of him.

He plucked up enough courage after a while to attempt to implore the driver to slow down. He turned to look at the man beside him. What he saw took the words out of his mouth. It wasn't so much the sight of him, although that was bad enough. He was the hairiest creature Tommy had seen in his life. A wild thatch of hair grew over his head and down over his ears, and was met by a long grizzled beard that almost covered his face and blew in the wind as if it had

life of its own. But that wasn't what struck Tommy dumb. With all that hair in the way Tommy could not be sure of it, yet he'd have sworn the man was grinning at him. Tommy didn't like it. He felt that grin was full of a peculiar sort of evil, and it gave Tommy such a queer feeling that he hurriedly turned away without saying a word.

Just at that moment the road made a turn and he saw at the side of it, a little distance ahead, a great stone gateway. Tommy knew from the stationmaster's description that it was the entrance to his friend's place.

He gave a great sigh of relief. "Pull up!" he cried to the driver. "This is where I get out."

But the driver made no sign of stopping, and the horse went racing past the gate. Tommy rose in his seat, shouting, "Stop!" Just then the cartwheels hit some obstruction in the road and Tommy, taken unawares, lost his balance. Over the side of the cart he flew and landed in the road on his hands and knees. By the time he pulled himself together and got to his feet, the cart was out of sight, although he could still hear the horse's hooves pounding down the other side of the hill.

Tommy would have liked to have had a chance to tell the fellow exactly what he thought of him, but it was too late for that. The cart was gone, and Tommy's bag had gone with it, but at least he hadn't paid the driver. Taking what comfort he could from that, Tommy limped back to the gateway, and up the drive to the door of his friend's house.

Tommy's friend was terribly surprised when he opened the door at Tommy's knock, and saw him standing there on the doorstone. But when he saw the plight Tommy was in he asked no questions. He hurried Tommy up to his room and saw that he had a good hot bath and found him some dry clothes to put on.

When Tommy came downstairs again, warm and dry and feeling a hundred times better, he was so relieved to have arrived safely that he was prepared to treat his whole experience as a joke. He handed over the telegram and told his friend he didn't think much of the telegraph service in the Highlands.

Tommy's friend had several other guests staying with him and they all gathered around Tommy now to hear the story of his mishap.

"Och, Tommy lad," said his friend. " 'Tis a long road and a bad night for walking."

"Did you walk all the way?" asked one of the guests.

"Well, no," said Tommy. "But I wish that I had. I got a lift from one of your wild Highlanders. I never had such a ride in my life before and I hope that I never shall again. And to top it all, the fellow went off with my bag."

"I wonder who it would be?" asked Tommy's friend. "Not many would be traveling in weather the like of this at night. The road is bad enough at best. A bit of rain makes it terrible."

"I'll grant you that," said Tommy. "The fellow was driving a tilt cart."

"A tilt cart!" exclaimed another man. "Och, they're none so common hereabouts. The only one I call to mind is the one belonging to auld Rabbie MacLaren."

"Now that you mention it, I remember," said Tommy. "That was the name of the man the stationmaster told me to have a care for. I suppose he meant that I was to keep out of his way. How I wish I had!"

There was a dead silence for all of five minutes. Then Tommy's friend asked, "What sort of man was he to look at, Tommy?"

"An old man, I'd say," Tommy told him. "He had more hair on his head and face than I've ever seen on a human being before. It probably looked like more than there really was of it, because it was so tangled and matted. Of course it was too dark for me to see much of him."

"What was the horse like, Tommy?" asked his friend.

"Not what you'd call a big beast," Tommy answered. "In fact he was somewhat on the small side. But how he could go! That horse would make a fortune on a race track. We bumped and thumped along at such a pace that I expected both wheels to fly off at any minute."

" 'Twas auld Rabbie MacLaren, to be sure!" said the guest who had asked about the tilt cart. "He was always one to be driving as if the de'il himself was after him. There's a bad spot a mile further on, over the hill. If you miss the road on the turn there, over the cliff you go to the glen below. Auld Rabbie came tearing along hell-bent one stormy night and missed the turn and went over."

"Went over!" Tommy exclaimed. "It's a wonder he wasn't killed!"

"Killed?" repeated the other man. "Of course he was killed. Auld Rabbie's been dead for a dozen years."

It took Tommy a minute or two to get through his head what he was being told. Then all of a sudden he understood.

"Dead!" screeched Tommy. *"Then I've been riding with a ghost!"* and he fainted dead away.

The next morning one of the gillies brought Tommy's bag up to the house to see if it belonged to anyone there. He'd found it lying in the glen at the foot of the cliff, below the road. It was the good stout sort of bag that is strapped as well as locked, so all the harm that had come to it was a scratch here and there.

Tommy had recovered from his fright by that time, so they took him out and showed him the place where auld Rabbie went over. They told Tommy he was lucky that he left the cart where he did, for when it got to the bad spot the tragedy was always re-enacted and over the cliff again went the old man with his cart and his horse. There had been some folks who got a ride with auld Rabbie, expecting to reach the village over beyond the next hill, who had found themselves below the road in the glen instead. A number of them had been badly hurt, and two or three had never lived to tell the tale.

Tommy suffered no ill effects from his experience. To tell the truth, he was rather proud of it. And as he took his fishing seriously, he didn't let the ride with auld Rabbie spoil his holiday. He stayed on to the end and fished all the streams in the neighborhood, and had a wonderful time.

But for a long time after he went home to London he couldn't sleep well on stormy nights. As soon as he turned out the light and closed his eyes he started to dream that he was riding wildly over that rough stony road in the tilt cart with the ghost of auld Rabbie MacLaren.

six

the man who helped carry the coffin

There's many a wonderful sight to see in the north of Scotland. There's the great causeway that's every bit as fine as the one in Ireland that the Irishers brag about. There's John O'Groat's house, and the high cliffs with the caves in them and the tides rushing in and out of them down below. The misty rocky isles where the seals gather to sing together are well worth the journey to see them, although if you wish to hear them you must keep well off the shore, for if the seals catch sight of you they'll slip into the sea and sing no more. But if you should happen to be up north in the springtime, there's another grand sight you'll not want to be missing, and that's the herring run at the town of Wick.

There's a sight which, once seen, you'll never be forgetting. There's all the stir and commotion of folks come for the fishing from up and down the coast and even from the Highlands and the islands. They all come pouring into the town to get their chance at a share of the fish. The harbor's that full of fishing boats loaded with shining fish coming in, and going out empty for another load, that you'd wonder where there'd be room for them all. Och! 'Tis a wonderful sight to see!

But just bide there till the run is over and folks from all the far places have gone back to their homes with their pockets full of the money from selling the fish they caught and their hearts light with the thought of it. There's something more than the fishing for you at the town of Wick, if you'll take the trouble to find it. And that's the harvest of curious tales the fisherfolk have gathered along with their fish.

Go down to the quay after the run is over and you'll find the brown nets spread to dry and the boats drawn up on the shore or riding at anchor in the quiet harbor. The fishermen that belong to the town will still be there. Some of them will be mending their nets or tidying their boats. And there will be some of them lounging lazylike about the taverns or the piers in little groups, just standing and talking. Now you'll get nowhere at all by just walking up to them and asking if any of them could tell you a tale or two. If you do, they'll melt away like morning mist before the sun, all having affairs to attend to elsewhere. The way to go about it is to step up to a group of them and ask for the kindness of a light for your pipe. They'll never refuse you that, but give it gladly. Then you could pass your sack of tobacco about to show your manners. They won't mind your standing about with them a while, talking about the fishing run that's just over and maybe admiring a boat or two. Give them time enough to get used to you and make up their minds about

you. If they take to you, they'll likely begin to talk as freely as if you were one of themselves. That's when you'll hear the grand old tales! Like as not you'll hear the one of how Andrew MacQuarrie helped to carry the coffin.

Andrew MacQuarrie was not a man who followed the sea himself. Being a crofter and the son of a crofter and the grandson of a crofter, he took no part in the fishing nor wanted any. But Andrew had a cousin Jamie, from down near Dornoch, who came up every year when the herring run was on to go out with the fishing boats and catch his share of fish, and considered himself well paid for the trouble of coming.

Jamie always liked to poke a bit of fun at Andrew about the fishing.

"Och, now!" he'd say. "Look ye here, Andy! Come along out in the boat wi' me. Why, lad, one season of the fishing will gi'e ye more good money than yon poor wee croft o' yours will make ye in five years!"

But Andrew only smiled and shook his head. "Thank ye kindly for your concern wi' my affairs, Jamie," he'd answer. "It is well meant, I dinna doubt. But keep to your boat, lad, and I'll keep to my croft. To my way of thinking, the sea's mischancy."

Then the two of them would laugh together and go on being as good friends as ever with no offense taken on either side.

Five or maybe six years went by like that, with Andrew's cousin coming up each year to stay with Andrew for the fishing season, and Andrew always happy to have his company. The last of these years was the best of them all. The fish seemed to leap into the nets as if wishing to be caught. Although the catch was the biggest any man could remember, yet the price paid was high because of the fine quality of the fish.

Jamie came back from selling his last boatload walking as proud as a gamecock and very full of himself.

"Take a look for yourself, Andy," he cried joyfully as he emptied the money from his pockets on the table. "Ha'e ye no regrets at all that ye stayed behind toiling on your croft for a wee bit o' siller and me making money wi' the fishing hand over fist?"

"Nay," said Andy placidly. "The croft is well enough. It suits me fine."

"Aye!" said Jamie, laughing at him. "And the sea's mischancy, as you say."

" 'Tis that," Andrew agreed. "What it gives it often takes away again. You can have your siller from the sea for all of me."

Jamie gathered up his money and stowed it away again in his pocket. "Mischancy or no, I'll say a good word for the sea," he said. "She gave us a fine run of herring this year and no mistake about it."

"Maybe so," said Andrew. "But I'd liefer put my trust in the land."

"Och, we'll ne'er agree!" cried Jamie. "Me for the sea and you for the soil. Well, the fishing is over for this time, so I'll be off home tomorrow."

Jamie planned to leave after noonday dinner. He spent the morn at the shore cleaning his nets and going over his fishing gear and stowing all in his boat for the journey home. He had finished and was back at the croft well before noon.

As they sat at table eating their dinner Andy asked suddenly, "Will ye not stay over a day or two, Jamie?"

"Stay over? Och, nay, I cannot do so. I'm packed and ready to go," Jamie said.

"I'm be glad o' your company," Andrew told him.

Jamie looked up from his plate in surprise. 'Twas not like Andrew to press him to stay. He'd ne'er done so before.

"Ye'd ha'e little o' my company," laughed Jamie, "and you off and away, busy on the croft all the day. Nay, lad, I've been long enough away from home."

Andrew said no more, but when dinner was over he said, "I'll walk down to the shore with you, Jamie, and see you off, then."

Jamie was more surprised than ever. 'Twas not like Andrew, either, to leave his work in the middle of the day. But he was fond of Andrew, so he accepted the offer gladly.

As they were walking down to the harbor Jamie noticed

that Andrew's face was troubled. "What's amiss, Andy?" he asked.

"Och, 'tis naught," said Andrew. But presently he added, "I do not like the look o' the sky or the feel o' the air, that's all. But maybe 'tis only a fancy I have."

"You're daft, man!" cried Jamie. "The sky is as clear and as blue as sky could be. And who could ask for a sweeter, fresher breeze?"

"The sky is too clear for my taste, and the breeze too uncertain. I'm not liking the feel of the weather," Andrew insisted.

"Crofter's notions," scoffed Jamie. So Andrew said no more.

It was not so easy for Jamie to get away as he had expected. There were fisherfolks galore from other places thronging the quay and harbor all getting ready to leave for their homes, too. Jamie had left some business to take care of later, thinking to be able to do it quickly just before he sailed. He had forgotten that dozens of others would be doing the same thing. Then there were friends to bid goodbye to, and take a *deoch an doruis* with for luck. So time wore on.

Andrew went along with Jamie wherever his fancy took him. As hour after hour slipped away he grew more uneasy. The tide seemed extra high and the waves were short and choppy while the winds blowing across them seemed to send them in several directions all at the same time. The church tower clock had long struck five before Jamie had wound up his business and finished taking leave of his friends.

Andrew plucked at his cousin's sleeve to draw his attention. "Ye'll ne'er be leaving, and it so late, Jamie," he said anxiously. " 'Twill be black night long ere you reach home."

"Havers!" Jamie said. "I'll have the moonlight to sail by. 'Tis the full of the moon. 'Twill be light as the day."

Well, if Jamie was set on going, there was no use for Andrew to waste his breath trying to hold him. But there was a queer brassy look to the sky where it met the water and the birds were flying low and inland from the sea. A sure sign of bad weather breeding, as anybody knew.

The two cousins shook hands and said farewell. Jamie stepped into his wee dinghy and started off for his fishing boat. Andrew waited until Jamie had set his sails and started off, tacking against the changing winds. Then he turned from the quay and walked into the town.

He met there with a man who had an ailing cow and had been coming to fetch Andrew to have a look at it. Andrew had a reputation for being knowledgeable about animals, and he liked the creatures anyway, so he went with the man willingly although the journey would take him several miles from home in the other direction.

He came out of the byre some hours later but he left the cow doing well behind him. He found night had fallen black with neither star nor moon to it. The farmer's wife stood in the light of the open door of the house.

"Did ye e'er hear such a doirionn!" she cried to them. "Och, 'twas a racketing old gale, to be sure!"

"We heard naught at all," Andrew said.

"Ye'd need to be deaf to miss it," the farmer's wife said. " 'Twas the biggest blowing I've ever known, wi' a great wind howling in frae the sea, and it roaring and whistling! It dinged down the two big trees by the burn above on the hill with a crash like the crack o' doom. Are ye telling me that neither o' ye heard it at all? I wondered that ye did not come running out to see."

"Nay," said Andrew. "We were busy tending the cow. I heard naught. But then I wasn't listening, my mind being on the poor beast."

"Nor I," said the farmer.

"Men!" said the farmer's wife in disgust. "There was half an hour and more of howling gale, wi' the world well nigh flying to pieces before it. And they hear naught but the groans of an ailing cow!"

She offered Andrew a bite of supper, but now that Andrew had heard about the storm he was anxious to get back home to make sure that all was well there. He borrowed a lantern to light him through the darkness and started off.

As he went across the town he could see signs of the damage the wind had done. There were broken chimney pots lying in the streets and even the bricks of a whole chimney now and then. He grew more and more anxious about his croft, so he went along as briskly as he could. He came at last to the end of the town where the lane that led to the croft came in at the crossroads. Just ahead of him there he saw some men, and they were carrying something big and making heavy work of it.

The lantern gave little light, but enough for him to see when he came up closer that there were three men and what they were carrying was a coffin.

There was nothing strange in that, for there was a kirk with a graveyard by it up the hill on the other road. Folks from the place who went to foreign parts and died there often had themselves sent back to be buried here at home. If it was more convenient to do so they were buried at night sometimes.

When Andrew came up to the men he saw that what was causing their trouble was that there were only three men, and it takes four men to carry a coffin properly, one at each corner. The way it was now with them, one man was trying to manage the end of it all alone. Andrew being good-hearted, he set his lantern down at the corner of his lane and stepped up to them.

"Ye're needing another man for yon job," said he. "I'll gi'e ye a hand to it."

The man at the end stepped over at once, and Andrew

put his shoulder under the fourth corner of the coffin. They
started off up the road to the kirk.

The uphill road was terribly steep and rough and the
coffin seemed to grow heavier at every step. 'Twas a very
good thing that they'd had his help, Andrew thought to
himself. The three of them could never have got it there
without him.

When at last they came to the kirk they went around
the side of it and laid the coffin down there in the kirkyard.
The three men stood there side by side, facing Andrew.

"Thank ye kindly," said the first man.

"Thank ye kindly," said the second man.

"Thank ye kindly," said the third.

"Och, 'twas no trouble at all," said Andrew. Then he
saw some spades lying on the ground by the coffin. Each man
now picked one of them up. "Gi'e me one o' the spades,"
said Andrew, "and I'll help with the digging o' the grave."

"We have but three," said the first man.

"We need but three," said the second man.

"Leave the digging be," said the third.

Andrew hesitated for a minute. It seemed unmannerly
not to help with the digging since he had helped with the
carrying.

While he stood there, not liking to insist on helping but
feeling it would only be neighborly to do so, the clouds
lifted and the full moon shone out between them. The clear

moonlight picked out the name plate on the coffin and Andrew, curious to know who he had been helping to carry to his grave, leaned over to read the name on the coffin plate. It struck him so queer when he read it that he had to read it over again. It didn't make sense the first time. It read:

JAMES MacQUARRIE
AGED TWENTY-NINE
DROWNED IN DORNOCH FIRTH

There was a date, too, but it was too small for Andrew to make out.

"Now, is it not a queer thing!" said Andrew. "I have a cousin named James MacQuarrie and him just twenty-nine years of age himself! Who'd ever think there'd be two lads of the very same name and age?"

He looked up at the three men standing by the coffin to see if they thought it strange, too. It had been too dark to see their faces before, but now in the moonlight he saw them plain. They were three brothers, neighbors of Andrew's and very good friends of Jamie's. And every last one of them had been drowned together the year before when their boat turned over in Pentland Firth during the herring run.

"Och, Jamie's drowned and dead!" cried Andrew and turned to run from the place. He knew that these were the coffin-walkers who had come from their watery graves to carry the ghost of the coffin of Jamie MacQuarrie, who had drowned in the gale that night.

To this day he could not say how he got down the hill. The first thing he remembers is sitting in the kitchen of the croft saying over and over, "Jamie's drowned and dead!".

He went up to the kirkyard the next day to see if maybe he had been wrong. But there was no sign of any new grave there, and nothing to show that there was a second James MacQuarrie aged twenty-nine, in the place. He talked to folks about it and they all agreed that it had happened the way he said, and that Andrew MacQuarrie had helped the three drowned brothers' ghosts carry the ghost of his cousin's coffin up the hill to the kirkyard.

Nobody was surprised, and least of all Andrew, when word came a little later that Jamie's boat had been found floating upside down and empty in Dornoch Firth and no trace of Jamie anywhere at all.

"Wasn't it just what we were expecting?" everybody said.

Well, you'll have to admit that Andrew was right about it. He always said the sea is mischancy and what she gives, she often takes away.

seven

the ghost that didn't want to be a ghost

There used to be a Glasgow man who was in the way of keeping a house for travelers beyond the town on the Great Western Road. He was a grand one for telling tales of ghosts and eerie happenings, and could keep at it for hours at a stretch, or at any rate as long as he had breath enough left to tell them with. He made a point of never telling a story unless he could swear to it that it was the solemn truth. He'd tell the place and date it happened and the name of the man or woman it happened to so that anyone could go and prove it for himself. He had a great liking for one story and told it often, about a ghost that didn't want to be a ghost. He said he got the story from the ghost of the old chief in the story. The old ghost used to stop in to keep him company now and then when the Glasgow man was all alone in his place. The Glasgow man could take you into the town and show you the very house where it happened, because he knew the lad in the tale when he himself was a lad.

The way it happened was that there was a clan of ghosts under an old Highland chief—one of the MacDonalds, no doubt. At any rate he was a fine old ghost and when he was a living, breathing man he had a great reputation for keeping all the clansmen and tenants under him well in hand and making them like it into the bargain. When he got over into the spirit world he used the same methods. They put a lot of ghosts under him there for him to be chief of, and it worked very well. In no time at all he had them taking their condition out-of-life as something that couldn't be helped and making the best of it. He even got them to feeling a certain pride and satisfaction in being ghosts and doing all they could to make a success of their work.

Everything was going along fine and easy, with every ghost of them busy and happy and the old chief proud of them all, when a new young ghost was sent over to take his place among them. It didn't take the ghosts of the old Chief's clan long to find out that he was not one of their kind at all.

The fellow was always moping about in corners. He refused to find a place of his own to haunt, and when they went to the trouble of finding one for him, he didn't like it at all. You never met such a ghost for complaining. There was naught in the place that he couldn't find something wrong with. He said the house he was haunting in was too dark and damp and dismal, and it made him ache all over. He said he didn't care for the color of his shroud, it being such a dirty shade of gray. He said that he didn't see why he should bother to go out haunting when there was such a lot of them that seemed to enjoy doing it while as for himself he found no pleasure in it at all. Then there were those chains they all had to carry around and clank. They were far too heavy, he told them. Anyway, why fash themselves with chains? Och, 'twas all a pack o' nonsense!

They tried to reason with him but it did no manner of good. He said he'd not asked anyone to let him be a ghost and he'd not be pretending he liked to be one. He got very rude about it and told them to go on about their ghosting and just leave him be.

So he just went along moping and complaining and wandering about aimlessly, getting into the way of the other ghosts and tripping them up because they were all too busy to notice that he was underfoot.

He was taking all the fun out of it for the rest of them, and at last they decided that it was too much to be borne. So they got up a petition to hand to the chief. It was a grand legal-looking paper having been drawn up by one of them who had been a solicitor in Glasgow before he happened to get to be a ghost. It stated their grievances against the discontented ghost and asked the chief to give his attention to relieving them.

The old chief was so put out when he got the petition that he turned two or three shades paler. He felt so queer that he even looked over his shoulder at the window to see if day was coming, although he knew quite well that it had just turned midnight. It really did upset him. The like of it had never happened to him before in one world or the other.

So he sent for the discontented ghost and gave him the petition to read for himself.

"What's come over you, lad?" roared the old chief. "What do you mean by setting the clan and all by the ears! You're putting the place in such an uproar that we'll be getting a bad name."

"It's not me," said the young ghost sulkily. "It's them. They're always nattering at me about bracing up and being a proper ghost."

"Well, why do you not do so then?" the old chief asked. "That would stop their nattering."

"Because I don't want to be a ghost at all!" cried the discontented ghost. "I never did want to be a ghost, either before or after I was one. I cannot thole it."

The answer struck the old chief dumb. He'd never met such a thing before. He really didn't know what to say. But before he'd gathered his wits together the young ghost cried out in despair, "Can't I be something else instead of a ghost? Is there not something you can do about it?"

The old chief had not headed two clans in two worlds without getting a very good knowledge of both human and ghost nature. This was not a matter he could settle by cajoling or arguing. He took a minute or two to think it over.

"Aye," said the old chief at last. "I'd not be saying that what you ask is impossible. But you'll have to understand that it's not myself that has the last word. I'll have to be getting permission. I'll do the best I can. Go along now, and be a good lad. I'll let you know."

It was maybe a matter of a week before the chief sent for the discontented ghost again. "Well, lad," he said cheerfully, as soon as the young ghost came into the room. "I'm to go ahead and find you something to suit you. I've been putting a lot of thought on the matter. How would it be if you just went back and were yourself again?"

"Well, I do not know about that," said the young ghost doubtfully. "After all, it's been a long time since I left and they've got used to me being gone. Besides, folks might not like the idea of me coming back to life again."

"Och, they'd like it fine! They'd jump at the chance to have you back," declared the old chief. "But there's no need for haste. I'll tell you what to do. Just go and look things over on the quiet and see for yourself."

So the young ghost did. He was back before the week was over.

The old chief greeted him hopefully. "I'm thinking you'll want to be leaving soon for home again," he said. "We'll have to be getting you ready for it."

"Och, nay!" the young ghost replied. " 'Twould never do at all. They've let my next younger brother have my room, and he's moved all his things into it with mine. The room's so full it's a regular dustbin, but the lad's daft about it. You see, it's the first time he's had a room all to himself because there were so many of us at home. I'd not have the heart to go back and take it from him."

"Then there's my job. They've given that to the young fellow I was breaking in. Och, the lad's got a young wife and a new bairn. I'd not want to go back and take the job from him. 'Twould not be fair at all."

"Was there not a lass you were thinking to marry?" asked the chief.

"You need not fash yourself about that," said the young ghost with a smile. "She'll be marrying my best friend soon. I'd not want to break that up."

The old chief looked shocked.

"It's a very good thing," the young ghost hastened to reassure him. "You see, it's this way. When I was living there were things I never noticed about her, but being away and going back again I saw things that I'd never bothered about before. I'll grant you she's a bonny lass. They don't come bonnier. But she's an awful one to be talking. I can see now that she talks a lot too much, and she says such silly things. My friend doesn't seem to mind it, but I could never put up with it. I'd be glad to go back for the sake of my mother and my father. They'd welcome me back, for I know them if I went back. What would the neighbors say? Besides, they love me and miss me. But it would bring trouble galore on if something happened to me again, they'd just have all the grief of losing me to suffer all over. Nay, I'll not go back."

"There's nothing we can do but put you in with somebody that's already in the world, then," said the old chief. "I'm warning you that it will not be comfortable at first, having to fit yourself in with somebody else. You'll be finding yourself feeling awful crowded until you get yourself used to it."

"I'd not be minding that," the young ghost said.

"Well, what would you have a fancy for?" asked the chief. But nothing he mentioned pleased the young ghost. A doctor? They could probably find a doctor to tuck him into.

"Nay, you'll not do that!" the discontented ghost exclaimed. He knew all about doctors. His father was one. Up at all hours of the night, they were, with never a chance at a whole meal any day of their lives, and hardly time to get acquainted with their own bairns. He'd not want anything to do with the law, either, for he couldn't take it upon himself to decide who was right or wrong. Farmers were all right, and he'd always liked the countryside, but they led such lonely lives and worked too hard. Being a schoolmaster wouldn't be too bad. He'd always liked bairns and had hoped to have a half dozen of his own. But a schoolmaster was always having to make his lads do things they didn't want, like being quiet and sitting on hard benches and not squirming around. Besides masters and lads seldom could make friends with each other. It was as if there were a wall between them and neither could get over to the other side.

Well, that was the way it went, with the old chief mentioning one thing after another, and the young ghost turning each suggestion down. At last the old chief suggested wearily, "Maybe you'd fancy being a financier?"

The young ghost brightened up. "That might suit me fine," he cried. "It would be grand to have money galore. But I'd like to go and make sure I'd like it before I decided."

"Go ahead," said the old chief, thankful to be rid of him for a time at least.

But the discontented ghost was back in a day or two.

"There couldn't be anything worse!" he told the chief. "Making a lot of money is fine enough, but the men who make it have to be running around so hard all day making it, and then they all lie awake all night worrying about losing it, so it ends up with their getting dyspepsia and nervous headaches and the like till they go nearly daft. I'd not be suited at all with that sort of life."

"Well, I've nothing more to offer," said the old chief. "I've reached my wits' end. Can you not think of anything yourself?"

"I'd not be saying I can at the moment," the young ghost replied. "But I'll try. I'll go and look around a bit." And he went away, leaving the old chief feeling so glad to see him go that he felt like a new ghost.

It was quite a long time before he came back again and the old chief had to look at him a couple of times before he recognized him. The air of discontent had dropped from him entirely and he was as joyful as any ghost could be.

"I've got it!" he cried. " 'Tis just the place for me!"

"Good!" the old chief exclaimed. "And what is it, then?"

"I want to be a cat!" announced the young ghost.

"A *cat!*" The old chief couldn't believe his ears.

"Aye, a *cat*." And looking into the old chief's face the young ghost begged. "Och, do not tell me I cannot! I've set my heart upon it."

"Och, nay!" The old chief hastened to say. " 'Tis not that it can't be done. To be sure though, a cat's an awful wee bit of a thing and it may take some trouble to fit you into it, but we could do it. As long as you're sure it's what you want."

"I'm sure enough. What's more, I know well the very cat I want to be," said the young ghost.

He led the old chief down through the streets of the town to a house that stood on a quiet square. They went into the house and up into a bedroom. The room was dark except for a lamp that stood on a table near the bed. There was a wee lad in the bed. He had been very ill and had got over his illness, but there was so little interest in life left in him that he just lay quietly and patiently, and there seemed to be nothing that could rouse him at all. His mother and father watched him from either side of the bed, keeping their eyes upon his face and hoping he'd show some notice of them. The young ghost paid no attention to the people in the room. He led the chief to the foot of the bed and pointed to a kitten that lay there sleeping on the blanket, curled up into a small furry ball.

"That's it," he said. "It wandered up here from the Broomielaw yesterday and they took it in and brought it up here to see if the bairn would like it. There's nine good lives in that wee body and it has the makings of a grand cat in it. That's the cat for me!"

The old chief said not a word, but he rolled up the sleeves of his shroud and, raising his bony arms, began making passes over the head of the young ghost.

The mother and father never noticed the two ghosts standing at the foot of the bed. And presently there was only one ghost there. The young ghost was gone. The old chief turned from the bed and went away.

Then the young ghost, as soon as he knew that he was all in the kitten, and really *was* the kitten himself, with four fine legs to leap about on and two fine ears to twitch and a fine long tail to swish, was so full of joy and delight that he began to dance at the foot of the bed. The thumping of the kitten's feet drew the lad's attention. He stirred and opened his eyes and looked at the kitten as it leaped and twisted and turned. The lad watched for a minute and the light came back into his eyes. He pulled himself up on his pillow and sat and pointed at the dancing kitten. And he laughed! 'Twas a weak sort of laugh and hardly worth the name, but it was a happy one. The kitten was the first thing he'd taken notice of for weeks and he was enchanted with it!

The bairn's mother caught the kitten up and kissed it on its little black nose and the bairn's father rang for the cook and had her bring it a bowl of cream. The doctor came and said that undoubtedly the kitten had saved the lad's life. There never was a kitten so petted and spoiled before.

The lad grew better and better and after a while was well and went out again to play with his companions. The cat grew bigger and bigger and became a most rampraring and uproarious young tomcat. He was adored by all the tabby cats for miles around and was the terror of all the other tomcats in the town. He lost one of his ears and the tip of his tail and eight of his lives in battle, but he was always careful to save the ninth life so as to be having one for his old age.

And when at last he died, full of years and still pampered and cossetted because of the ancient service he had done the family when he saved the bairn's life, he gave up his last life most contentedly and willingly.

That was because of something he had known about cats from the very beginning. Since they are given nine lives to live, they live them all out in this world. Cats don't have ghosts!

eight

the lads who met the highwayman

There was a barrister lived in Edinburgh who was so matter-of-fact and dry as dust that a body'd never have believed that anything out of the way could ever have happened to him. But one night when he was sitting in company after dinner, and talk began to go around about strange things they'd heard, one of the men at the table remarked that it was queer that nobody ever heard such a tale from the person directly concerned in it but always at second-hand or even third-hand.

The barrister spoke up at that and said that there was one experience that he could tell them at first-hand. He could vouch for the truth of it himself, because it happened to him and one of his brothers when they were lads still going to school.

His age at the time was about fourteen and his brother was a year younger. As lads will at that age, they were beginning to feel that they were old enough to do a bit of planning for themselves. The summer holidays when they'd be out of school were close at hand, so they decided they'd like to take a trip somewhere together just to do and see something different for a change. Barring a trip or two to the seashore when they were very small, they'd never been far from Edinburgh. Like many Scottish folks, their parents had acquired a good-sized family and little money to tinkle in their pockets, as time went on. So most of their pleasures were homemade and their outings were seldom farther than their legs would carry them. When there are half a dozen lads and a couple of lassies in a family to feed and clothe and give an education, there's never any money left to pay for junketing away from home for holidays.

The father of the lads had a younger brother who had a good-sized croft in the Highlands. The lads had never seen the croft, and they thought it would be a grand plan to go and visit this uncle until school took up again. They had it all figured out well beforehand. So when they got out of school and were back home they went and asked their father if they could.

"You'll not need to be laying out a penny for us," the older lad told him proudly. "We've been saving all year from our pocket money and we have plenty to pay both our fares, up and back again."

"Besides," the younger brother put in, "you'll be in pocket whatever you'd have laid out for our keep while we were at home. You'll save that clear, if we go."

It amused their father quite a bit to find them so businesslike, but he kept a straight face and treated the matter seriously.

"I can't see that I'll be saving anything at all," he objected. "I'll have to be paying your uncle for your keep."

"You'll not have to be doing that," the lads assured him, "for we'll be working on the croft for our keep."

Their father saw that they had it well thought out. It did not sound unreasonable, though he was not sure how much their work would be worth to their uncle. He told them he was willing for them to go providing that their uncle was willing to have them come.

So they wrote and told their uncle that if he'd let them come and stay until school took up again, they'd earn their keep at whatever work he set them to do.

Their uncle wrote back that they might come as soon as they pleased and stay as long as they liked. He'd be glad to have a couple of pairs of extra hands to help him. So the whole family got to work getting their clothes ready and packing them up, and off the two lads went to the croft in the Highlands.

Being town-bred they had plenty to learn and were kept busy. But they learned quick and, as they were willing and neither lad was lazy, before very long they proved to be of real use to their uncle. They liked their aunt and their uncle and were liked in return. On the whole, the life suited them. They were glad they had come.

Their uncle particularly enjoyed having them about. He had no bairns of his own and he regretted it sorely. So he treated the lads as if they had been his own sons, taking care that they were not idle yet not working them too hard, and making sure that they had a reasonable amount of free time for themselves. He was still young enough to remember what it was like to be a lad, so he put them in the way of having any sort of enjoyment that could be had.

One day their uncle's shepherd told them there were going to be some dog trials at the market town six miles away on the coming Saturday. They'd heard often about dog trials, but had never had an opportunity to see any; so they set their hearts on going as soon as the shepherd told them. They went to their uncle and asked his leave to be off from their work on Saturday so that they could walk over to the town to see the dogs at work.

"Och!' said their uncle thumping his head with his fist. "And me for a dumb ox! I meant to tell you we'd be going on Saturday but I forgot. There's no need for you to be walking. We'll go in the cart." So early on the Saturday the lads and their uncle went off to town.

It was a wonderful day for the lads. They'd never have believed that dogs could be so knowing. The way they rounded the sheep up, turning them this way and that way, and sending them wherever they ought to go with no more sign from the shepherd than a lifted finger or maybe a nod of the head was amazing. The dog that belonged to their uncle's shepherd came off with a prize which made the lads almost burst with the pride of it. When all was over they came back from the field to the town fair blazing with excitement.

As they reached the edge of the town they saw that a fair had pitched its booths there. At once the lads were at their uncle. Could they not just go and have a look at the fair? After such a grand day the fair would be the best sort of end to it.

Their uncle shook his head. He must get back to the croft. The men would see to things, no doubt, but he must go about the place to make sure naught was left undone. He could not wait for them to carry them back in the cart, he told them.

"We weren't expecting it," they told him. "We'll not mind walking."

Their uncle regarded them doubtfully for a while, but then said, "Och, ye'll be taking no harm from it." He put his hand in his pocket and drew out his purse.

"I doubt you'll be leaving the fair till the last booth's taken down and folded away. So mind this!" he said as he gave them some money. "I'll not have you traveling on the Sabbath Day. If you find you've not left enough time to get back home well before midnight, you'll have to stay until Monday in the hotel. And have a care that you attend the kirk here morning and evening, should you stay!"

Before they could thank him properly he had rattled

ghosts *go haunting*

off in the cart. They had a bit of money of their own, for
their father had sent them their pocket money, just as he
always did when they were at school. So they put the money
their uncle had given them in the older lad's purse and he put
it carefully away in an inside pocket so as to be sure it was
extra safe. Then they crossed the field and came up to the fair.

It was none so big but it had most of the usual things
you find in fairs. There was a roundabout and a giant swing
and a small switchback to ride upon. There were half a dozen
booths with freaks and tumblers and the like, and a coconut
shy. But it pleased the lads anyway. (Still a fair like that does
not take long for one to tire of it.) After they'd made the
rounds of it several times the lads were ready to leave. They
went into the town and found the hotel. But what with the
folks who had come for the dog trials, and were staying so as
not to travel on the Sunday, and those who were in the town
on other business, there was no room left for the lads. It was
only half an hour after nine and still not dark. Six miles does
not seem so long when you are at the beginning of it, so the
two of them decided to start to walk back to the croft. They
were both used to walking and they'd get there well before
midnight.

The first couple of miles they went along larking about
as lads will do and playing tricks on each other. The excitement of the day had not worn off and they were pleased at
the thought of giving back to their uncle the money he'd

given them for the hotel. But before they were more than
half way back night had fallen. They began to feel the length
of the road they must still cover. The croft seemed a far
way off. So they settled down to a steady jog and just trudged
along. After a long while they came to the kirk where they'd
be going with their aunt and uncle in the morning. Their
hearts lightened then, for there was only a little better than
a mile left to travel. They were pretty sure there'd be a bit of
supper kept back for them, just in case they came in, and it
would be welcome. But what would be even more welcome
was their bed. Losh! How tired they were! They agreed,
talking it over, that the day had been too much for them.

"I don't feel able for the hill," said the elder lad.

"Nor I," sighed the younger.

Just beyond the kirk was a crossroad where the road from
Edinburgh crossed the sideroad they were traveling by. The
high road was a good hard road and once there had been a lot
of going back and forth on it, what with the mail coach and
the stage coach and a sluagh of grand folks in their carriages,
but the railroad had long ago put an end to all that. Under the
moon the road lay empty now at either side, and their own
road lay as empty before them. They started across the high-
way to take the road up the hill that led to their journey's end.
They were halfway over before they noticed that there was
something big and dark under the great oak tree at the right
on the far corner of the roads. Maybe a tinker's van or a

broken-down cart, they thought, not caring very much
because of the weariness in them. But when they got closer
they saw that it was a huge black horse. The horse was so
dark that it was almost hidden in the shadow under the tree.
Then they saw that it bore a man upon its back. The man
was as dark as the horse, for he wore a long black cloak and a
soft wide-brimmed hat as black as the cloak and the horse.
The lads both thought it was a strange-looking pair to be
meeting in that place at that hour, but they gave him a polite
"Good e'en" and made to pass by on their way. Then they

stopped dead in their tracks. In answer to their greeting the man brought both his hands up from under his cloak and in each hand was a long black pistol. The lads stood stock-still, too terrified to move. The pistols were the old-fashioned kind that were seldom seen nowadays, but they had a terribly businesslike look to them. Then the man spoke, in a quiet, easy voice that was as frightening as the pistols. "I'll have what money you've got, my friends," said the man, "and look sharp about it!"

All the money the lads had left was what they were carrying back to their uncle, but they didn't stop to argue with the man. The older lad made haste to pull his purse from his pocket and he hurled it with all his might at the dark stranger. The man caught it deftly but the lads did not wait to find out if he was satisfied with the contents. The two of them took to their heels and fairly flew up the hill. The wind itself would have been put to it to keep up with them. They ran till they reached their uncle's house and burst through the doorway and tumbled over each other into the room where their uncle and aunt were sitting, having a quiet cup of tea before going off to bed.

Their uncle set down his cup with a crash and jumped up from his chair. "What's amiss with you, lads?" he cried in alarm.

"We've been robbed!" cried the older lad, getting his breath at last.

"It was a man all in black on a big black horse," panted the younger lad. "He was down by the oak at the crossroads."

"He held a pair of pistols on us and asked for our money. We were bringing what you gave us back to you, but I just pitched the purse at him and then we ran. 'Tis a shame we lost it for you," the older lad said regretfully.

"Maybe he'll be coming after us," his brother said fearfully.

Their uncle stared at them for a minute. Then he burst into a roar of laughter. He sat down in his chair again and took up his cup of tea. "Och!" he told them. " 'Tis plain to see that you've been getting acquainted with the ghost of our highwayman!"

"Ghost!" the lads exclaimed.

"Aye," said their uncle. "I've ne'er seen the fellow myself, but I know many a one that has. He'd ne'er do you any harm."

"But he looked so real," the lads protested.

"He has not been real for a hundred years or more," the uncle told them. "Och, he was a slippery one. They were hard put to lay hands on him. But they nabbed him at last. It turned out that he was a well respected gentleman from the town. He'd always been a decent-seeming quiet sort of a body with plenty of money. It gave them a turn when they found where he was getting it from. They caught him right there at the crossroads and, after he'd been tried at the assizes, they brought him back and hanged him right there where they caught him. He's buried there, too. 'Twas the custom in those days. You could have kept your purse in your pocket and walked right past him. He'd not have harmed you at all."

"But he has the money," insisted the older lad. "He caught the purse in his hand."

"Maybe so," said his uncle. "Come now! Eat up your piece and drink your tea. 'Tis close on midnight. By the looks of you, you're needing your sleep the night."

Well, when they walked down to kirk next morn, there was the purse in the grass under the oak tree at the crossroads. Their uncle picked it up and handed it to them. "Your highwayman had no need for your money," he said with a smile. "You'd best keep it for yourselves. You've earned it."

When they went back to Edinburgh at the end of their holidays they had a grand story to tell all their friends and you may be sure they made the most of it.

It wasn't the last they saw of the croft, for the two brothers went back every summer to lend their uncle a hand. For that matter they still do, for they've taken the place of sons to their uncle and aunt. But although they have traveled up and down the hill a hundred times or more, they have never again met up with the ghost of the highwayman.

nine

how tammas macivar macmurdo
maclennan met his match

If there e'er was a man in Scotland from the border to John o' Groat's who had no notion of what it was like to be scared, it was Tammas MacIvar MacMurdo MacLennan. He said as much himself. Maybe it wasn't far off from the truth when you took the matter into consideration. Everybody agreed to that. Wasn't it Tammas himself who mastered MacKail's big fierce bull when it broke out of the field and came tearing down the village street bellowing and snorting and sort of daring anybody to get in his way? All the rest of the village folks ran for cover and slammed their doors behind them, and nobody would have held it against Tammas if he had done the same. Tammas stood fast and let the bull come at him. When the bull was close enough, Tammas just stepped aside and before it could get its head down to gore him Tammas had caught the beast by the tender part of its nose and sort of leaned his weight against it. The bull stopped short and when folks peeped out of their windows thinking to see Tammas a gory sight adangle from the bull's horns, all they saw was Tammas leading the bull back to pasture by its nose, and the creature going along with Tammas peaceably and unresisting.

Then there was that day when one of MacLaren's hounds took offense at something that was done by Jamie MacInness' big hound Ron. The MacLaren dog leapt for Ron, but Ron was ready for him. In the space of a minute you couldn't tell head from tail, or which hound was which. Such snarling and growling and snapping of teeth you never heard in your life. The women and bairns stood weeping and the men circled about and shouted and cursed. But they took great care to keep out of the range of the field of battle. Just at the moment who should turn into the street but Tammas, stepping lightly and easily along as he always did. He didn't even lose a step but came on steady right up to the dogs and pitched right in. The dogs were so busy trying to tear each other piecemeal that they never saw Tammas coming at them at all. Before they knew it, Tammas had grabbed the MacLaren dog by the scruff of the neck and pulled Jamie's Ron away from him. He gave the MacLaren hound a boot that sent him skirling halfway down the street. He gave Jamie's Ron a clout o'er the lugs before he cast him away. The hounds were fair sickened against the fight after Tammas took a hand in it. It ended right then and there with the two of them slinking off in opposite ways, with their tails tucked in between their legs.

Nobody could deny that Tammas was a man of remarkable courage. If sometimes he said so himself, it wasn't laid against him for bragging. Most folks said "Aye" to it without stopping to think twice. If there were some who thought "Maybe" they took good care not to say it out loud, Tammas having the edge on them when it came to heft and size. But it wouldn't be in the nature of some folks that they wouldn't be hoping that some fine day the doughty lad would meet his match and get a rare old fright. It would do Tammas good to be taken down a peg or two, they thought. Well, the time came when they got what they hoped for. Tammas hasn't lived it down to this very day!

It all came about because of MacInness's big hound, Ron. Jamie MacInness set great store by the creature. It was of the old true breed, the same that the pirates in the old days used to bring over from Ireland to sell. There were not many of the big dogs thereabouts and the way Jamie cherished it you'd be thinking 'twas made of gold. Ron was somewhat of a rover, as such big hounds are likely to be, and Jamie was always missing him and going in search of him.

"Have ye seen my Ron?" he'd be asking, day in and day out. So one evening Jamie came down to where the men in the village were gathered to have a bit of friendly talk, their day's work being done. 'Twas just between daylight and dark when Jamie came among them.

"Have ye seen my Ron?" he asked. "I've been seeking him high and low and not got sight or sound of him."

"Maybe the tinkers made off with him," said one of the men.

"Och, there's not been a tinker about for weeks," said Jamie. "Ron was home this morn."

"Is he not somewhere on the moor?" another asked. "Ron's a great one for coursing after the hares."

"I've been," said Jamie. "He's not there at all. I went up to the copse where the fox's hole is, too, but he's not there, either."

"Did ye try MacLaren's?" someone suggested. "Ron's often off with MacLaren's hounds. When he's not fighting with one o' them."

"Fighting or friendly, he's not there," Jamie answered. "I've been up there to see."

"Did ye have a look up the glen?" asked Tammas.

"The glen! Och, nay! I'd not have the dare," exclaimed Jamie. "I'd ne'er go there by myself."

"What's wi' the glen?" asked Tammas, although he knew full well.

"There's ghaists to it," said Jamie with a shudder.

"Och, who's afeart o' ghaists?" scoffed Tammas, laughing.

"Me," Jamie said.

Everybody laughed with Tammas, but when Jamie asked if one of them would go into the glen with him to help search for Ron 'twas strange how all of them had pressing business in the other direction. One had to fetch his wee lass from her grannie's and another had an errand to do for his wife. Some said they were overdue for supper as it was, and their wives would have their ears off if they didn't hurry home. Every man of the lot had some excuse or other. All but Tammas.

"I'll go wi' ye, Jamie," said Tammas. "Come away, man." So the two of them went off to the glen to search for Ron.

They were well up the glen before they came across the missing hound. He was crouched before a badger's hole, the image of patience itself, and showing every intention of staying there until the badger came out of its den. The dog was not well pleased to be dragged away from his quarrie. Jamie had a struggle to get him collared and leashed. It took him some time, the dog being so unwilling. While Jamie was at it, Tammas walked along the stream a little farther up the glen. When Jamie came up to him with the leashed hound in hand, Tammas was looking up the glen toward its end. Tammas whispered, "Eist, Jamie! Look ye now! There's a light in the cliff up the glen."

It was a soft glow, rather than a light, and by the looks of it came from some opening in the wall of the cliff, perhaps a cave.

"Come away home," begged Jamie, tugging at Tammas' arm. "'Tis ghaists!"

"Ghaists, my foot!" Tammas whispered. "More likely men. Let's see what they're up to."

"If men, it's likely smugglers," protested Jamie. "They'll have our lives should they catch us."

"What way would it be smugglers?" Tammas asked in scorn. "Wi' the glen five miles from the sea and no way to get up it but straight through the village?"

"I'm going home," quavered Jamie.

"Go home if you like," Tammas told him. "But you'll go by yourself. I'm staying till I find out what's there."

Jamie looked back the way they had come. It was a long way down the glen to the village and it was filled with the darkness of night. Even with Ron beside him he did not like to go back alone. So Jamie went along with Tammas. He felt much safer as long as Tammas was with him. Nothing could daunt the doughty lad, Jamie thought to himself.

Their feet, being used to the ways of moor and mountain, made scarcely a sound as they crept up on the light using the caution they'd have taken in stalking a deer. When they came near the slit in the rock from which the light shone they stopped and listened. They could hear no sound from the cave at all. They couldn't see into the cave because they were pressing close to the cliff at the edge of the opening. Tammas felt around on the ground at his feet till he found a fair-sized rock, and this he pitched into the cave. They could hear the rock scudding and bouncing along the floor of the cave, with the echoes following after. When the stone stopped, everything was as silent as before.

"They're all off and away," said Tammas. "I'll wager it's some lads has a still for making mountain dew. Well, nobody's home the night. I'm going in." Into the cave he stepped with Jamie and Ron close behind him.

They took no more than a few short steps before they stopped dead in their tracks. For the life of them they could not have gone farther. The sight they saw fair nailed their feet to the floor.

The cave before their eyes was like the great hall of a castle. Along the walls were fastened torches all lit and flaming. That was where the light came from that they had seen in the glen.

The light from the torches shone down upon the figures of nine huge men and every man of them was twice as big as Tammas. They sat at a long stone table, three at the head and three on either side. All the men wore the dress of the ancient warriors and each had a narrow circlet of gold about his brow. Each man held a rusty claymore upright in one hand and with the other hand supported a shield. There were names on the shields in letters of gold. The names on the shields of the men at the head of the table were Angus, Fergus, and Lorne. The names on the other shields couldn't be read for the shields were turned away. All the men sat there silent and motionless, deep in sleep, with their heads bowed down on their breasts.

The hound, Ron, pressed against Jamie's legs and

whimpered. The man in the middle at the head of the table stirred but did not wake. Still deep in slumber, he asked, "Is it the time?"

It was not Tammas who answered. Tammas was so terrified he might have been turned to stone. He couldn't have said a word if it was to save his life. It was little Jamie MacInness who answered. "Not yet!" piped Jamie. "Nay, not yet!"

Jamie's voice brought Tammas back to himself again.

"Ochon a righ!" he shouted. "'Tis the ghaists of the auld kings of Dailriadagh!" and grabbing Jamie by the arm he rushed him out of the cave. "Let me out o' here!" cried Tammas. They were lucky to get out in time, for the opening of the cave slammed shut so close behind them that they could feel the wind of it banging to with a crash at their backs. If they'd been delayed for a minute they'd all have been caught and crushed to death.

Tammas was right about it. 'Twas the ghosts of the old kings, Fergus, Angus, and Lorne and their six sons sitting there in slumber as they had sat through hundreds of years, waiting for someone to come and call them back to battle.

The way Jamie tells the tale, Tammas dragged him and Ron back down the glen at such a wild speed that half of the time they were flying through the air, their feet not touching ground at all. He didn't stop for rock or burn or thicket but plowed right through them all. When they got clean down to the middle of the village Tammas stopped and dropped his hold on Jamie's arm. He looked at Jamie as if he'd ne'er seen him before in his life. Then he gave an eldritch screech and fell to the ground. Tammas lay there like a log and Jamie could not rouse him nor could he lift him. So he had to go and wake up the men of the village to get their help. They took a door off its hinges and loaded Tammas upon it. He was such a dead weight it took eight of them to bear him to his home.

Nobody saw hide or hair of Tammas for a long time. When he came back among them again nobody said a word about the matter. After all, Tammas still had the edge on them when it came to size and weight. But it was a sore burden to Tammas that everybody knew he had met his match. It sort of whittled him down to size. He couldn't say any more that there was nothing could daunt him. Not after he'd met the ghosts of the old kings in the glen.

the young irish lad from the hiring fair

Whenever times were bad in Ireland or the potato crop failed, young folks used to come over in droves to Scotland in the springtime to find work on the farms and crofts. Many an Irish family would have starved to death during the long cold winter had it not been for the wages these lads and lasses brought home after their serving time was over at summer's end.

In the old days most of the Scottish farming towns had hiring fairs where folks who wanted work would stand waiting to be hired. Farmers would go along the line looking them over and picking out the ones whose looks they liked.

There was a young Irish lad who came over from Galway one year in the springtime looking for farm work at the hiring fair. He'd never been there before in his life and he knew little about it. So when a farmer came along and made a bid for his services, he took the offer without stopping to think twice. He knew that according to the law of those days he'd get no pay until the harvest was gathered in, but then his master was bound to feed and keep him. Thinks the lad, 'tis six o'one and half dozen o' t'other. So the farmer gave him a penny to bind the bargain, and he was hired from planting time until harvest time, a matter of six months.

When they got to the farm the lad was showed the place he'd be going to sleep in. 'Twas a bit of a shed built on against the house and so small a man would almost have to go out of it to turn around in it. It held but a cot and a wooden stool, nor was there room for more.

"'Tis not a castle by any manner o' means," said the Irish lad. "But I'll make do."

Then they called him to supper and he found there was naught but oatmeal porridge with an onion or two on the side for spice. But he'd seen days at home in the starving times when there had been even less to eat.

"'Tis not a meal the king himself would fancy," said the Irish lad. "But as long as there's plenty of it I've naught against it."

As soon as he'd finished his supper the farmer told him to be off to his bed. He'd need his sleep for they rose early, the farmer said. The lad didn't know how early it was going to be, but it wasn't long before he found out. He'd hardly settled himself to sleep when the farmer thumped on the door and told him to get himself up and ready for work. The Irish lad could tell by the moon that daybreak was two hours or more away.

"They start the day early here indeed," he said. "Sure if they started out any earlier they'd meet themselves going to bed."

Well, that was the way the days went on. There was

porridge and onions for breakfast, dinner, and supper, and as soon as supper was over, then off to bed, only to turn out of bed again hours before the cock was making up his mind to crow. The farmer kept the lad working so hard that sometimes he felt that he was getting clear out of breath.

The only time he could call his own was Sunday. After the lad had fed and watered the stock and milked the cows and done the things that had to be done each day he was free to do as he pleased with the rest of the day. His master feared that his neighbors would make it hot for him if he made the farm lad work on the Sabbath Day. It irked the farmer sadly to see the Irish lad idle but there was naught he could do about it.

There were a couple of other Irish workers on the farms nearby and the lad made friends with them, but he saw little of them. The farmer called them good-for-naughts and chased them away whenever they showed their noses on his place. So the Irish lad spent most of his time on Sundays lying under the hedge and whistling to himself. He always whistled the same old tune for it was the only one he knew. The name of it was the "Londonderry Air."

'Twas no great wonder that the lad soon grew homesick. To be in Ireland again was the wish in his heart. The more he wished the more he whistled until he was whistling his one little tune all the whole day long.

The farmer didn't like the whistling nor did he care for

the tune. "Can you not hauld yer whisht?" he grumbled. "The whistling's driving me daft!"

"That I cannot," said the Irish lad. "The tune is all that I was able to bring over from Ireland with me. I couldn't keep it off my lips if I tried."

Well, the farmer didn't want to turn the lad off before the time they'd agreed upon was over. The hiring laws were strict about that. If a farmer sent a worker away when he'd put in but half of his time he had to pay him for all of it the same as if he'd worked it. The farmer wasn't going to put his hand in his pocket and pay him for six months when he'd only worked three. So the lad stayed on.

The lad grieved for Galway and whistled the "Londonderry Air," and the farmer listened because he couldn't help it.

The only bright spot in the Irish lad's life was the young wife of the farmer. Her heart was touched by his sorry plight. She'd slip him an extra piece to eat when the farmer wasn't around to see, and she'd listen to the lad talk about Ireland when he wasn't around to hear it. But she had to be careful that the farmer didn't catch her at it. The man didn't know the meaning of kindness himself. He'd have made her suffer for it if he caught her being kind to the Irish lad.

When the three months were well over the lad had had enough. He went to the farmer and asked him to let him have what he'd earned so far and let him go. But the farmer would not do it. This time he had the hiring laws on his side. If a worker went away before the time that he had agreed to work was over, the farmer could keep his wages for the whole six months.

"Go if you like," said the farmer. "I'll not stop you. But if you quit of your own accord, you'll get not a penny of your pay no matter how long you've worked, unless you've put in every day from planting time to harvest. That's the law of it, my lad!"

"Och," said the Irish lad. "Listen now to reason! Have I not worked for you early and late and never shirked for better than three months? Give me my pay for a month of it and I'll not ask for more. That way you'll have two good months of my work that you'll not be paying a penny for. All I ask is enough for my fare to carry me back to Galway."

"I'll give ye nothing at all," the farmer said.

The young Irish lad flew into a rage. "I'll tell you this!" he said. "If you make me stay when I'm so heartsick to go, I'll be likely to die of it. And if I do, it's myself will come back to haunt you, so I will!"

The farmer roared with laughter at that. "Get on with your work," said he, "and waste no more time."

The lad whistled and worked his way through the rest of the week until Sunday. When Sunday came he finished his chores and went off somewhere on his own. He was not seen for the rest of the day and the farmer hoped he had gone for good, but he hadn't. Back he came at bedtime. He told them he wasn't feeling so well and off he went to his bed.

Well, the farmer went early to call him in the morning, but he got no answer at all when he banged on the door. So he opened the door and peered into the room. It was dark and quiet and he could not hear the sound of anyone breathing. Maybe the amadan's gone off, he said to himself. But he went to the bed to make sure. It was too dark to see but he leaned over the bed and felt around in it. The lad was there all right. But under the farmer's hand he lay so stiff and still that the farmer was seized with fright.

"Ochon, he's dead!" he cried. He ran out of the room and cried to his wife that the Irish lad was lying dead on his bed and himself was off to the village to fetch the doctor.

When the farmer came back with the doctor the two of them went into the shed. The bed was empty and the lad was gone!

"The de'il's in it!" shouted the farmer. "He never could have moved himself for he was as stiff and dead as a stone."

"There were a couple of men came asking for him after you were gone," said the farmer's wife. "I told them where to find him. Happen they took him away with them. I wouldn't know. I didn't go into the shed with them for I was busy putting the porridge over the fire for your breakfast."

"A couple of men!" exclaimed the farmer. "Who would they be?"

"They looked to be Irishers," his wife answered. "It was not long they stayed. I heard them going away, but I did not see them."

Well, there were no two ways about it, the farmer decided then. The Irish lad's friends had come to see him and when they found him lying there dead they'd carried him away with them. So he was saved the cost of burying him. But he had to pay the doctor for his trip. The farmer was put out about that, seeing the doctor had not laid eyes on the Irish lad at all. But the doctor was even angrier at being brought out on a fruitless errand, so he made the farmer pay for it before he went away.

The farmer had to work alone that morning. But he did not mind the double load at all. He was not ill-pleased with the way things had turned out for him in spite of the doctor's fee. He was in pocket a tidy sum since he had three months of the lad's wages and half the season's work well done. If he could find another lad he'd only have to pay half as much as he had expected to in the beginning with only three months instead of six until harvest.

He was working in one of the far fields and at the thought he began to chuckle—but he stopped short. Someone, somewhere, was whistling! The tune was the "Londonderry Air!"

He looked about him in every direction, but all he saw anywhere was his wife with a basket on her arm, coming to fetch him his dinner.

"Did you hear somebody whistling?" he asked when she came up to him.

"I heard blackbirds up in the copse," she answered. "They were singing their heads off as I came along."

"Och, ye ninny! A blackbird does not whistle a tune!" the farmer told her. She said naught to that. So he snatched the basket from her arm roughly and sent her back home.

Wherever he was after that, by night or by day, he heard it. There was never anyone he could see, only what he could hear. He knew what it was. The Irish lad had come back to haunt him, just as he had said he would.

He would hear it as he sat at table, coming through the window from outside. "Do you hear naught?" he would ask his wife.

His wife would stop eating and listen. Then she would answer calmly, "Nay, I hear naught," and go on eating her dinner. "What is there to hear?" she would ask.

He took to going down to the village in the evenings to try to drown his fears in drink at the tavern. But even there the whistling followed him and it brought him back to his home again. Then after the Irish lad was gone three weeks or thereabouts, one night when the farmer was walking up the road he heard someone coming along behind him. He'd have thought it was a neighbor on his way home like himself had it not been that the one who followed was the one who was doing the whistling and keeping time to the tune with his feet as he came along. When the farmer slowed down, the follower did the same, and when the farmer went faster, the follower went faster, too. It made the farmer terribly uneasy. He was just on the point of making a run for home when a voice called out. "Stop, farmer! I want a word with you!"

It was the voice of the young Irish lad!

The farmer had not dared to cast a look behind him before, but now he had to do so. He couldn't help himself. The sight he saw made his blood grow cold and his hair creep on his head. The figure that stood in the road was as white as the misty moonlight that shone upon it. It was clad in the long white grave-clothes that folks wore when they were laid in their graves, and its hands and its face glowed like the false fire on old decayed wood in a bog. When the farmer last saw the Irish lad his hair had been red, but now it was long and white and the locks of it waved eerily when the night wind passed across it. There was no doubt in the farmer's mind at all. This was the Irish lad's ghost!

"What do you want wi' me, Irish lad's ghost?" quavered the farmer in a voice that was shaky and weak.

"There's the matter of a bit of money between us," said the Irish lad. "And I'll not be leaving you until justice is done me. There was a time when I'd have let you off cheap with a month's pay, but now I'll have my six month's wages you hired me at, and not a penny less."

"I've not got so much on me," protested the farmer

from between his chattering teeth. "My money's all in my money box under the bed at home."

The Irish lad's ghost gave a grisly laugh. "We'll go together and fetch it, then," he said.

"Och, nay!" shrieked the farmer. "I'll go by myself!" And off he tore up the road without waiting to see if the Irish lad's ghost was coming along. But he heard the Irish lad's voice calling after him. "Play me no tricks, my fine fellow," it said. "Locks and bars will not keep me out if I've a mind to come in."

It was all that was needed to put wings on the farmer's feet. He fairly flew up the road and into the house and slammed the door behind him. Straight to the money box he went and counted out the money he had agreed to pay the Irish lad for his six month's work. He crept back to the door and opened it to a crack just wide enough for him to thrust his hand through, and laid the money on the doorstone. He didn't look outside to see if the ghost was there to take it. He banged the door shut and barred it tight and then he leaped into bed, clothes, boots and all. He pulled the covers up over his head and lay there shivering and shaking.

His wife stared in amazement. She didn't know what was amiss with him, but she thought she could guess what had happened. She only shook her head and said, "Och, the man's gone daft!"

The Irish lad's wages were gone from the doorstone in

the morning. The farmer was gone from the house, too. So was all the rest of the money that he had kept in his money box. Nobody ever saw him again or knew where he had gone to, but there was a rumor that he had been seen getting into the London Coach when it stopped in the village at midnight. Wherever he went, daft or not, he'd had wits enough left to take the rest of his cash from the money box along with him.

His wife stayed at the farm for a while and waited to see if he was coming back. When he did not she sold everything up and took the money from it and went away herself.

About a year later a strange tale began to go about the neighborhood. A man from the village was the one who started the story going. He came back from working in foreign parts and he said that he had been one of the crew on a fishing boat that was taking some English gentlemen over to Ireland for the salmon fishing, and they had stopped in at a place in Galway. The man from the village said that the Irish lad was not dead at all, no matter what the farmer had told the doctor. The man said he could swear to the truth of what he was telling because with his own two eyes he had seen the Irish lad himself. The lad was sitting on a stone on the shore mending a salmon net and all the time he was working away at it, he was whistling that same tune he always used to whistle. The one they called the "Londonderry Air."

And as the man from the village was going along the road that led up from the shore, whom should he meet but the farmer's wife! She was wearing one of those scarlet petticoats that women thereabouts wear. Her feet were bare and she was carrying a creel of seaweed upon her head. She was stepping along, light and carefree, and upon her face was a happy smiling look that was ne'er seen upon it whilst she was living up at the farm. She passed him by in the road and she looked straight at him and through him, as if she'd ne'er seen him in her life before. But he knew it was her just the same. He'd even take his oath on it! If they didn't believe him they could go over to Galway and find out for themselves.

Well, some say 'twas all a clever trick that the Irish lad played on the farmer to get his money and some say 'twas the Irish lad's ghost that came back and frightened the farmer away. But as none of them ever went over to Galway to find out if what the man from the village told them was true or not, nobody knows the right of it up to this very day.

glossary

Some of the words in this list are "braid Scottish" and others are Gaelic. In order to show origin, Scottish words are followed by s and Gaelic words by g.

AMADAN (G) *ah-ma-dan* (sometimes spelled amaudhan). a foolish person

AULD (S) *awld*. old

BIDE A BIT (S) wait a while

BOTHAN (G) *bŏ´awn*. a small cottage or hut

BURN (S) a small stream or brook

BYE-LOW (S) (sometimes spelled balou). a lullaby

BYRE (S) a shed or barn for farm animals

CRACK O' DOOM (S) judgment day

CROFTER (S) a sheep farmer, usually holding his croft on leasehold from one of the great landlords

DAFT (S) crazy

DEASIL (G) *dy-asil*. (In the north the "de" in words approximates the sound of "j." Very probably it would sound like "jasil.") Clockwise, moving around an article or point from east to west and back again as the hands of a clock move.

DE'IL (S) *dee'il* (sometimes also, deh-il). devil

DEOCH AN DORUIS (G) *dy-ock an doe-ris*. a stirrup cup; a farewell drink; literally, a drink at the door

DINGED (S) slammed or banged down

DOIRIONN (G) *do-ir-on* a racket or hullabaloo

EIST! (G) *issht*. Listen!

ELDRITCH (S) weird, uncanny

FALADH-DHA (G) *fa-lá-y-há*. a trick, hoax or joke

FASH (S) worry, bother (Dinna fash yersel': that is, "Don't worry," or "Don't bother!")

GILLIES (S) menservants, also the men hiring out as guides for hunting and fishing

GREETING (S) crying; as, a greeting bairn, i.e., a crying child

HAULD YOUR WHISHT! (S) Hold your tongue! Be quiet!

HAVERING (S) talking foolishly

HAVERS! (S) Nonsense!

KIRK (S) church

KIRKYARD (S) churchyard

LIEFER (S) rather

MANSE (S) the dominie or minister's house, usually next door to the kirk

MISCHANCY (S) unlucky

NATTERING (S) arguing; nagging

OCHON A RIGH! (G) *Oo'n-a-ree.* literally, Oh, the king! an ejaculation of surprise equal to the English "Good lord!"

SASSENACH (G) *Sas-sen-ack.* Saxon, a name designating those who are not Highlanders, particularly the English.

SGREUCH (G) (sometimes spelled skreigh). a cry or shriek. sgreuch is pronounced *skrayck*; skreigh is pronounced *skray*

The sgreuch o' dawn; literally the cry o'dawn, means daybreak.

SHEILING (S) *sheeling.* a cottage

SILLER (S) silver; particularly, silver money

SKIRLING (S) whirling; spinning; dancing

SPEIRING (S) *speering.* asking; questioning.

TAKE A TELLING (S) listen to advice.

THOLE (S) to bear; to endure

TILT CART (S) a two-wheeled, light cart favored by Gypsies, it usually has a canvas cover, stretched over hoops of wood or steel.

WEANS (S) very small bairns

WHISHT! (S) Listen!

WULLY (S) short for William; English: variation Willie